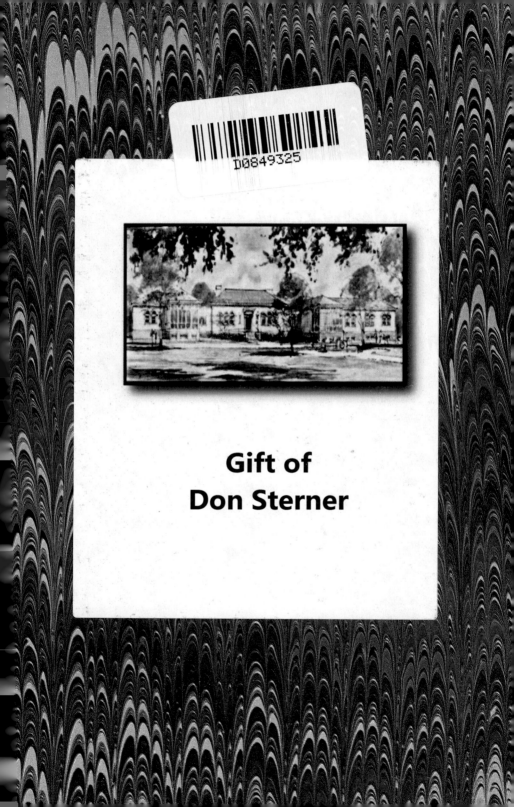

**Gift of
Don Sterner**

MURDER
IN
THREE ACTS

MURDER IN THREE ACTS

AGATHA CHRISTIE

BANTAM BOOKS
TORONTO • NEW YORK • LONDON • SYDNEY • AUCKLAND

MURDER IN THREE ACTS
A Bantam Book / published by arrangement with
Dodd, Mead & Company

PRINTING HISTORY
Dodd, Mead edition published in 1934
The Agatha Christie Mystery Collection / January 1988

If you would be interested in receiving bookends for The Agatha Christie Mystery
Collection, please write to this address for information:

The Agatha Christie Mystery Collection
Bantam Books
P.O. Box 957
Hicksville, New York 11802

ISBN 0-553-35069-2

PRINTED IN THE UNITED STATES OF AMERICA

0 9 8 7 6 5 4 3 2 1

CONTENTS

Directed by SIR CHARLES CARTWRIGHT.

Assistant Directors { MR. SATTERTHWAITE.
MISS HERMIONE LYTTON GORE.

Clothes by AMBROSINE, LTD.

Illumination by HERCULE POIROT.

FIRST ACT

SUSPICION

CHAPTER I

MR. Satterthwaite sat on the terrace of Crow's Nest and watched his host, Sir Charles Cartwright, climbing up the path from the sea. Crow's Nest was a modern bungalow of the better type. It had no half timbering, no gables, no excrescences dear to many a builder's heart. It was a plain, white, solid building, deceptive as to size, since it was a good deal bigger than it looked. It owed its name to its position, high up, overlooking the harbor of Loomouth. Indeed, from one corner of the terrace, protected by a strong balustrade, there was a sheer drop to the sea below. By road, Crow's Nest was a mile from the town. The road ran inland and then zigzagged high up above the sea. On foot it was accessible in seven minutes by the steep fisherman's path that Sir Charles Cartwright was ascending at this minute.

Sir Charles was a well-built, sunburned man of middle age. He wore old, gray-flannel trousers and a white sweater. He had a slightly rolling gait, and carried his hands half closed as he walked. Nine people out of ten would say, "Retired naval man; can't mistake the type." The tenth and more discerning would have hesitated, puzzled by something indefinable that did not ring true. And then perhaps a picture would rise unsought—the deck of a ship, but not a real ship—a ship curtailed by hanging curtains of thick, rich material—a man, Charles Cartwright, standing on that deck, light that was not sunlight streaming down on him, the hands half clenched, the easy gait and a voice—the easy, pleasant voice of an English sailor and gentleman—a great deal magnified in tone.

"No, sir," Charles Cartwright was saying, "I'm afraid I can't give you any answer to that question."

And swish fell the heavy curtains, up sprang the lights, an orchestra plunged into the latest syncopated measure, girls with exaggerated bows in their hair said, "Chocolates? Lemonade?" The first act of *The Call of the Sea*, with Charles Cartwright as Commander Vanstone, was over.

From his post of vantage, looking down, Mr. Satterthwaite smiled.

A dried-up little pipkin of a man, Mr. Satterthwaite, a patron of art and the drama, a determined but pleasant snob, always included in the more important house parties and social functions—the words "and Mr. Satterthwaite" appeared invariably at the tail of a list of guests. Withal, a man of considerable intelligence and a very shrewd observer of people and things.

He murmured now, shaking his head, "I wouldn't have thought it. No, really, I wouldn't have thought it."

A step sounded on the terrace, and he turned his head. The big, gray-haired man who drew a chair forward and sat down had his profession clearly stamped on his keen, kindly, middle-aged face. "Doctor" and "Harley Street." Sir Bartholomew Strange had succeeded in his profession. He was a well-known specialist in nervous disorders and had recently received a knighthood in the birthday-honors list.

He drew his chair forward beside that of Mr. Satterthwaite and said: "What wouldn't you have thought, eh? Let's have it."

With a smile, Mr. Satterthwaite drew attention to the figure below, rapidly ascending the path.

"I shouldn't have thought Sir Charles would have remained contented so long in—er—exile."

"By Jove, no more should I!" The other laughed, throwing back his head. "I've known Charles since he was a boy. We were at Oxford together. He's always been the same—a better actor in private life than on the stage! Charles is always acting. He can't help it; it's second nature to him. Charles doesn't go out of a room; he 'makes an exit,' and he usually has to have a good line to make it on. All the same, he likes a change of part—none better. Two years ago he retired from the stage—said he wanted to live a simple country life, out of the world, and indulge his old fancy for the sea. He comes down here and builds this place. His idea of a simple country cottage. Three bathrooms and all the latest gadgets! I was like you, Satterthwaite. I didn't think it would last. After all, Charles is human; he needs his audience. Two or three retired captains, a bunch of old women and a parson—that's not much of a house to play to. I thought the 'simple fellow with his love of the sea' would run for six months. Then, frankly, I thought he'd tire of the part. I thought the next thing to fill the bill would be the weary man of the world at Monte Carlo, or possibly a laird in the highlands—he's versatile, Charles is."

The doctor stopped. It had been a long speech. His eyes were full of affection and amusement as he watched the man below. In a couple of minutes he would be with them.

"However," Sir Bartholomew went on, "it seems we were wrong. The attraction of the simple life holds."

"A man who dramatizes himself is sometimes misjudged," pointed out Mr. Satterthwaite. "One does not take his sincerities seriously."

The doctor nodded.

"Yes," he said thoughtfully, "that's true."

With a cheerful hallo, Charles Cartwright ran up the steps onto the terrace.

"*Mirabelle* surpassed herself," he said. "You ought to have come, Satterthwaite."

Mr. Satterthwaite shook his head. He had suffered too often crossing the Channel to have any illusions about the strength of his stomach afloat. He had observed the *Mirabelle* from his bedroom window that morning. There had been a stiff sailing breeze, and Mr. Satterthwaite had thanked heaven devoutly for dry land.

Sir Charles called for drinks.

"You ought to have come, Tollie," he said to his friend. "Don't you spend half your life sitting in Harley Street telling your patients how good a life on the ocean wave would be for them?"

"The great merit of being a doctor," said Sir Bartholomew, "is that you are not obliged to follow your own advice."

Sir Charles laughed. He was still unconsciously playing his part—the bluff, breezy, naval man. He was an extraordinarily good-looking man, beautifully proportioned, with a lean, humorous face, and the touch of gray at his temples gave him a kind of added distinction. He looked like what he was—a gentleman first and an actor second.

"Did you go alone?" asked the doctor.

"No"—Sir Charles turned to take his drink from a smart parlormaid who was holding a tray—"I had a hand. The girl Egg, to be exact."

There was something—some faint trace of self-consciousness—in his voice which made Mr. Satterthwaite look up sharply.

"Miss Lytton Gore? She knows something about sailing, doesn't she?"

Sir Charles laughed rather ruefully.

"She succeeds in making me feel a complete landlubber, but I'm coming on, thanks to her."

Thoughts slipped quickly in and out of Mr. Satterthwaite's mind:

"I wonder . . . Egg Lytton Gore. . . . Perhaps that's why he hasn't tired of the place. She's very attractive."

Sir Charles went on, "The sea—there's nothing like it. Sun and wind and sea, and a simple shanty to come home to."

And he looked with pleasure at the white building behind him, equipped with three bathrooms, hot and cold water in all the bedrooms, the latest system of central heating, the newest electrical fittings and a staff of parlormaid, housemaid, chef, and kitchenmaid. Sir Charles's interpretation of simple living was, perhaps, a trifle exaggerated.

A tall and exceedingly ugly woman issued from the house and bore down upon them.

"Good morning, Miss Milray."

"Good morning, Sir Charles. Good morning." A slight inclination of the head toward the other two. "This is the menu for dinner. I don't know whether you would like it altered in any way."

Sir Charles took it and murmured:

"Let's see. Melon cantaloupe, borscht soup, fresh mackerel, grouse, *soufflé Surprise, canapé Diane.* . . . No, I think that will do excellently, Miss Milray. Everyone is coming by the 4:30 train."

"I have already given Holgate his orders. By the way, Sir

Charles, if you will excuse me, it would be better if I dined with you tonight."

Sir Charles looked startled, but said courteously:

"Delighted, I am sure, Miss Milray, but—er——"

Miss Milray proceeded calmly to explain: "Otherwise, Sir Charles, it would make thirteen at table. And so many people are superstitious."

From her tone, it could be gathered that Miss Milray would have sat down thirteen to dinner every night of her life without the slightest qualm. She went on:

"I think everything is arranged. I have told Holgate that the car is to fetch Lady Mary and the Babbingtons. Is that right?"

"Absolutely. Just what I was going to ask you to do."

With a slight, superior smile on her rugged countenance, Miss Milray withdrew.

"That," said Sir Charles reverently, "is a very remarkable woman. I'm always afraid she'll come and brush my teeth for me."

"Efficiency personified," said Strange.

"She's been with me for six years," said Sir Charles. "First as my secretary in London, and here, I suppose, she's a kind of glorified housekeeper. Runs this place like clockwork. And now, if you please, she's going to leave."

"Why?"

"She says"—Sir Charles rubbed his nose dubiously—"she says she's got an invalid mother. Personally, I don't believe it. That kind of woman never had a mother at all. Spontaneously generated from a dynamo. No, there's something else."

"Quite probably," said Sir Bartholomew, "people have been talking."

"Talking?" The actor stared. "Talking what about?"

"My dear Charles, you know what talking means."

"You mean talking about her—and me? With that face? And at her age?"

"She's probably under fifty."

"I suppose she is." Sir Charles considered the matter. "But seriously, Tollie, have you noticed her face? It's got two eyes, a nose and a mouth, but it's not what you would call a face—not a female face. The most scandal-loving cat in the neighborhood couldn't seriously connect scandal with a face like that."

"You underrate the imagination of the British spinster."

Sir Charles shook his head.

"I don't believe it. There's a kind of hideous respectability about Miss Milray that even a British spinster must recognize. She is virtue and respectability personified, and a useful woman. I always choose my secretaries plain as sin."

"Wise man."

Sir Charles remained deep in thought for some minutes. To distract him, Sir Bartholomew asked:

"Who's coming this afternoon?"

"Angie, for one."

"Angela Sutcliffe? That's good."

Mr. Satterthwaite leaned forward interestedly, keen to know the composition of the house party. Angela Sutcliffe was a well-known actress, no longer young, but with a strong hold on the public, and celebrated for her wit and charm. She was sometimes spoken of as Ellen Terry's successor.

"Then there are the Dacreses."

Again Mr. Satterthwaite nodded to himself. Mrs. Dacres was Ambrosine, Ltd.—that successful dressmaking establishment. You saw it on programs: "Miss Blank's dresses in first act by Ambrosine, Ltd., Bruton Street." Her husband, Captain Dacres, was a dark horse, in his own racing parlance. He spent a lot of time on race courses—had ridden himself in the Grand National in years gone by. There had been some trouble—nobody knew exactly what, though rumors had been spread about. There had been no inquiry, nothing overt, but, somehow, at mention of Freddie Dacres people's eyebrows went up a little.

"Then there's Anthony Astor, the playwright."

"Of course," said Mr. Satterthwaite, "she wrote *One-Way Traffic*. I saw it twice. It made a great hit."

He rather enjoyed showing that he knew that Anthony Astor was a woman.

"That's right," said Sir Charles. "I forget what her real name is—Wills, I think. I've only met her once. I asked her to please Angela. That's the lot—of the house party, I mean."

"And the locals?" asked the doctor.

"Oh, the locals! Well, there are the Babbingtons; he's the

8

parson; quite a good fellow, not too parsonical, and his wife's a really nice woman. Lectures me on gardening. They're coming—and Lady Mary and Egg. That's all. . . . Oh, yes, there's a young fellow called Manders; he's a journalist, or something. Good-looking young fellow. That completes the party."

Mr. Satterthwaite was a man of methodical nature. He counted heads.

"Miss Sutcliffe, one; the Dacreses, three; Anthony Astor, four; Lady Mary and her daughter, six; the parson and his wife, eight; the young fellow, nine; ourselves, twelve. Either you or Miss Milray must have counted wrong, Sir Charles."

"It couldn't be Miss Milray," said Sir Charles, with assurance; "that woman's never wrong. Let me see. Yes, by Jove, you're right. I have missed out one guest. He'd slipped my memory." He chuckled. "Wouldn't be best pleased at that either. The fellow is the most conceited little devil I ever met."

Mr. Satterthwaite's eyes twinkled. He had always been of the opinion that the vainest men in creation were actors. He did not exempt Sir Charles Cartwright. This instance of the pot calling the kettle black amused him.

"Who is the egoist?" he asked.

"Rum little beggar," said Sir Charles. "Rather a celebrated little beggar, though. You may have heard of him. Hercule Poirot. He's a Belgian."

"The detective," said Mr. Satterthwaite. "I have met him. Rather a remarkable personage."

"He's a character," said Sir Charles.

"I've never met him," said Sir Bartholomew, "but I've heard a good deal about him. He retired some time ago, though, didn't he? Probably most of what I've heard is legend. Well, Charles, I hope we shan't have a crime this week-end."

"Why? Because we've got a detective in the house? Rather putting the cart before the horse, aren't you, Tollie?"

"Well, it's by way of being a theory of mine."

"What is your theory, doctor?" asked Mr. Satterthwaite.

"That events come to people, not people to events. Why do some people have exciting lives and other people dull ones? Because of their surroundings? Not at all. One man may travel to the ends of the earth and nothing will happen

9

to him. There will be a massacre a week before he arrives, and an earthquake the day after he leaves, and the boat that he nearly took will be shipwrecked. And another man may live at Balham and travel to the City every day, and things will happen to him. He will be mixed up with blackmailing gangs and beautiful girls and motor bandits. There are people with a tendency to shipwrecks—even if they go on a boat on an ornamental lake, something will happen to it. In the same way, men like your Hercule Poirot don't have to look for crime; it comes to them."

"In that case," said Mr. Satterthwaite, "perhaps it is as well that Miss Milray is joining us and that we are not sitting down thirteen to dinner."

"Well," said Sir Charles handsomely, "you can have your murder, Tollie, if you're so keen on it. I make only one stipulation—that I shan't be the corpse."

And, laughing, the three men went into the house.

CHAPTER II

THE principal interest of Mr. Satterthwaite's life was people. He was, on the whole, more interested in women than in men. For a manly man, Mr. Satterthwaite knew far too much about women. There was a womanish strain in his character which lent him insight into the feminine mind. Women all his life had confided in him, but they had never taken him seriously. Sometimes he felt a little bitter about this. He was, he felt, always in the stalls watching the play, never on the stage taking part in the drama. But, in truth, the rôle of onlooker suited him very well.

This evening, sitting in the large room giving onto the terrace, cleverly decorated by a modern firm to resemble a ship's cabin *de luxe,* he was principally interested in the exact shade of hair dye attained by Cynthia Dacres. It was an entirely new tone—straight from Paris, he suspected—a curious and rather pleasing effect of greenish bronze. What Mrs. Dacres really looked like, it was impossible to tell. She was a tall woman, with a figure perfectly disciplined to the demands of the moment. Her neck and arms were her usual shade of summer tan for the country; whether naturally or artificially produced it was impossible to tell. The greenish-bronze hair was set in a clever and novel style that only London's best hairdresser could achieve. Her plucked eyebrows, darkened lashes, exquisitely made-up face, and mouth lipsticked to a curve that its naturally straight lines did not possess, seemed all adjuncts to the perfection of her evening gown of a deep and unusual blue, cut very simply, it seemed—

11

though this was ludicrously far from the case—and of an unusual material—dull, but with hidden lights in it.

"That's a clever woman," thought Mr. Satterthwaite, eyeing her with approval. "I wonder what she's really like."

But this time he meant in mind, not in body.

Her words came drawlingly, in the mode of the moment: "My dear, it wasn't possible. I mean, things either are possible or they're not. This wasn't. It was simply penetrating."

That was the new word just now—everything was "penetrating."

Sir Charles was vigorously shaking cocktails and talking to Angela Sutcliffe, a tall, gray-haired woman with a mischievous mouth and fine eyes.

Dacres was talking to Bartholomew Strange: "Everyone knows what's wrong with old Ladisbourne. The whole stable knows."

He spoke in a high, clipped voice—a little, red, foxy man with a short mustache and slightly shifty eyes.

Beside Mr. Satterthwaite sat Miss Wills, whose play, *One-Way Traffic*, had been acclaimed as one of the most witty and daring seen in London for some years. Miss Wills was tall and thin, with a receding chin and very badly waved fair hair. She wore pince-nez and was dressed in exceedingly limp green chiffon. Her voice was high and undistinguished.

"I went to the South of France," she said. "But, really, I didn't enjoy it very much. Not friendly at all. But, of course, it's useful to me in my work—to see all the goings-on, you know."

Mr. Satterthwaite thought: "Poor soul. Cut off by success from her spiritual home—a boarding house in Bournemouth. That's where she'd like to be." He marveled at the difference between written works and their authors. That cultivated man-of-the-world tone that Anthony Astor imparted to her plays—what faintest spark of it could be perceived in Miss Wills? Then he noticed that the pale-blue eyes behind the pince-nez were singularly intelligent. They were turned on him now with an appraising look that slightly disconcerted him. It was as though Miss Wills were painstakingly learning him by heart.

Sir Charles was just pouring out the cocktails.

"Let me get you a cocktail," said Mr. Satterthwaite, springing up.

Miss Wills giggled.

"I don't mind if I do," she said.

The door opened and Temple announced Lady Mary Lytton Gore and Mr. and Mrs. Babbington and Miss Lytton Gore.

Mr. Satterthwaite supplied Miss Wills with her cocktail and then sidled into the neighborhood of Lady Mary Lytton Gore. He had a weakness for titles.

Also, apart from snobbishness, he liked a gentlewoman, and that Lady Mary most undeniably was.

Left as a widow very badly off, with a child of three, she had come to Loomouth and taken a small cottage, where she had lived with one devoted maid ever since. She was a tall, thin woman, looking older than her fifty-five years. Her expression was sweet and rather timid. She adored her daughter, but was a little alarmed by her.

Hermione Lytton Gore, usually known for some obscure reason as Egg, bore little resemblance to her mother. She was of a more energetic type. She was not, Mr. Satterthwaite decided, beautiful, but she was undeniably attractive. And the cause of that attraction, he thought, lay in her abounding vitality. She seemed twice as alive as anyone in that room. She had dark hair and gray eyes, and was of medium height. It was something in the way the hair curled crisply in her neck, in the straight glance of the gray eyes, in the curve of the cheek, in the infectious laugh that gave one that impression of riotous youth and vitality.

She stood talking to Oliver Manders, who had just arrived.

"I can't think why sailing bores you so much. You used to like it."

"Egg, my dear, one grows up."

He drawled the words, raising his eyebrows.

A handsome young fellow, twenty-five at a guess. Something perhaps a little sleek about his good looks. Something else—something—— Was it foreign? Something un-English about him.

Somebody else was watching Oliver Manders. A little man with an egg-shaped head and very foreign-looking mustaches. Mr. Satterthwaite had recalled himself to M. Hercule

Poirot's memory. The little man had been very affable. Mr. Satterthwaite suspected him of deliberately exaggerating his foreign mannerisms. His small, twinkly eyes seemed to say, "You expect me to be the buffoon? To play the comedy for you? *Bien,* it shall be as you wish!"

But there was no twinkle now in Hercule Poirot's eyes. He looked grave and a little sad.

The Reverend Stephen Babbington, rector of Loomouth, came and joined Lady Mary and Mr. Satterthwaite. He was a man of sixty-odd, with kind, faded eyes and a disarming, diffident manner.

He said to Mr. Satterthwaite: "We are very lucky to have Sir Charles living among us. He has been most kind, most generous. A very pleasant neighbor to have. Lady Mary agrees, I am sure."

Lady Mary smiled.

"I like him very much. His success hasn't spoiled him. In many ways he is"—her smile deepened—"a child still."

The parlormaid approached with the tray of cocktails as Mr. Satterthwaite reflected how unendingly maternal women were. Being of the Victorian generation, he approved that trait.

"You can have a cocktail, mums," said Egg, flashing up to them, glass in hand. "Just one."

"Thank you, dear," said Lady Mary meekly.

"I think," said Mr. Babbington, "that my wife would allow me to have one."

And he laughed a little gentle, clerical laugh.

Mr. Satterthwaite glanced over at Mrs. Babbington, who was talking earnestly to Sir Charles on the subject of manure.

"She's got fine eyes," he thought.

Mrs. Babbington was a big, untidy woman. She looked full of energy and likely to be free from petty-mindedness. As Charles Cartwright had said—a nice woman.

"Tell me." Lady Mary leaned forward. "Who is the young woman you were talking to when we came in—the one in green?"

"That's the playwright, Anthony Astor."

"What? That—that anaemic-looking young woman? Oh"—she caught herself up—"how dreadful of me! But it was a surprise. She doesn't look—I mean she looks exactly like an inefficient nursery governess."

It was such an apt description of Miss Wills's appearance that Mr. Satterthwaite laughed. Mr. Babbington was peering across the room with amiable shortsighted eyes. He took a sip of his cocktail and choked a little. He was unused to cocktails, thought Mr. Satterthwaite amusedly; probably they represented modernity to his mind, but he didn't like them. Mr. Babbington took another determined mouthful with a slightly wry face and said:

"Is it the lady over there? . . . Oh, dear——" His hand went to his throat.

Egg Lytton Gore's voice rang out, "Oliver, you slippery Shylock——"

"Of course," thought Mr. Satterthwaite, "that's it—not foreign—he's Jewish!"

What a handsome pair they made. Both so young and good-looking, and quarreling too. Always a healthy sign.

He was distracted by a sound at his side. Mr. Babbington had risen to his feet and was swaying to and fro. His face was convulsed.

It was Egg's clear voice that drew the attention of the room, though Lady Mary had risen and stretched out an anxious hand.

"Look," said Egg's voice. "Mr. Babbington is ill."

Sir Bartholomew Strange came forward hurriedly, supporting the stricken man and half lifting him to a couch at one side of the room. The others crowded round, anxious to help, but impotent.

Two minutes later, Strange straightened himself and shook his head. He spoke bluntly, aware that it was no use to beat about the bush.

"I'm sorry," he said. "He's dead."

CHAPTER III

"COME in here a minute, Satterthwaite, will you?"
Sir Charles poked his head out of the door.

An hour and a half had passed. To confusion had succeeded peace. Lady Mary had led the weeping Mrs. Babbington out of the room and had finally gone home with her to the vicarage. Miss Milray had been efficient with the telephone. The local doctor had arrived and taken charge. A simplified dinner had been served, and by mutual consent the house party had retired to their rooms after it. Mr. Satterthwaite had been making his own retreat when Sir Charles had called to him from the door of the ship room, where the death had taken place.

Mr. Satterthwaite passed in, repressing a slight shiver as he did so. He was old enough not to like the sight of death. For soon, perhaps, he himself—— But why think of that?

"I'm good for another twenty years," said Mr. Satterthwaite robustly to himself.

The only other occupant of the ship room was Bartholomew Strange. He nodded approval at the sight of Mr. Satterthwaite.

"Good man," he said. "We can do with Satterthwaite. He knows life."

A little surprised, Mr. Satterthwaite sat down in an armchair near the doctor. Sir Charles was pacing up and down. He had forgotten the semi-clenching of his hands and looked definitely less naval.

"Charles doesn't like it," said Sir Bartholomew. "Poor old Babbington's death, I mean."

16

Mr. Satterthwaite thought the sentiment ill expressed. Surely nobody could be expected to "like" what had occurred. He realized that Strange had quite another meaning from the bald one the words conveyed.

"It was very distressing," said Mr. Satterthwaite, cautiously feeling his way. "Very distressing indeed," he added, with a reminiscent shiver.

"H'm—yes, it was rather painful," said the physician, the professional accent creeping for a moment into his voice.

Cartwright paused in his pacing.

"Ever see anyone die quite like that before, Tollie?"

"No," said Sir Bartholomew thoughtfully. "I can't say that I have. But," he added in a moment or two, "I haven't really seen as many deaths as you might suppose. A nerve specialist doesn't kill off many of his patients. He keeps 'em alive and makes his income out of them. MacDougal has seen far more deceases than I have, I don't doubt."

Doctor MacDougal was the principal doctor in Loomouth, whom Miss Milray had summoned.

"MacDougal didn't see this man die. He was dead when he arrived. There was only what we could tell him, what you could tell him. He said it was some kind of seizure; said Babbington was elderly and his health was none too good. That doesn't satisfy me."

"Probably didn't satisfy him," grunted the other. "But a doctor has to say something. 'Seizure' is a good word—means nothing at all, but satisfies the lay mind. And, after all, Babbington was elderly, and his health had been giving him trouble lately; his wife told us so. There may have been some unsuspected weakness somewhere."

"Was that a typical fit or seizure, or whatever you call it?"

"Typical of what?"

"Of any known disease."

"If you'd ever studied medicine," said Sir Bartholomew, "you'd know that there is hardly any such thing as a typical case."

"What, precisely, are you suggesting, Sir Charles?" asked Mr. Satterthwaite.

17

Cartwright did not answer. He made a vague gesture with his hand. Strange gave a slight chuckle.

"Charles doesn't know himself," he said. "It's just his mind turning naturally to the dramatic possibilities."

Sir Charles made a reproachful gesture. His face was absorbed, thoughtful. He shook his head slightly in an abstracted manner.

An elusive resemblance teased Mr. Satterthwaite, then he got it. Aristide Duval, the head of the secret service, unraveling the tangled plot of *Underground Wires*. In another minute he was sure. Sir Charles was limping unconsciously as he walked. Aristide Duval had been known as The Man with a Limp.

Sir Bartholomew continued to apply ruthless common sense to Sir Charles's unformulated suspicions:

"Yes, what do you suspect, Charles? Suicide? Murder? Who wants to murder a harmless old clergyman? It's fantastic. Suicide? Well, I suppose that is a point. One might, perhaps, imagine a reason for Babbington wanting to make away with himself."

"What reason?"

Sir Bartholomew shook his head gently.

"How can we tell the secrets of the human mind? Just one suggestion—suppose that Babbington had been told he suffered from an incurable disease, such as cancer. Something of that kind might supply a motive. He might wish to spare his wife the pain of watching his own long-drawn-out suffering. That's only a suggestion, of course. There's nothing on earth to make us think that Babbington did want to put an end to himself."

"I wasn't thinking so much of suicide," began Sir Charles.

Bartholomew Strange again gave his low chuckle.

"Exactly, Charles. You're not out for probability. You want sensation—new and untraceable poison in the cocktails."

Sir Charles made an expressive grimace.

"I'm not so sure I do want that. Remember I mixed those cocktails, Tollie."

"Sudden attack of homicidal mania, eh? I suppose the symptoms are delayed in our case, but we'll all be dead before morning."

"Damn it all, you joke, but——" Sir Charles broke off irritably.

"I'm not really joking," said the physician.

His voice had altered. It was grave and not unsympathetic.

"I'm not joking about poor old Babbington's death. I'm casting fun at your suggestions, Charles, because—well, because I don't want you, thoughtlessly, to do harm."

"Harm?" demanded Sir Charles.

"Perhaps you understand what I'm driving at, Mr. Satterthwaite?" ·

"I think, perhaps, I can guess," said Mr. Satterthwaite.

"Don't you see, Charles," went on Sir Bartholomew, "that those idle suspicions of yours might be definitely harmful? These things get about. A vague suggestion of foul play, totally unfounded, might cause serious trouble and pain to Mrs. Babbington. I've known things of that kind to happen once or twice. A sudden death, a few idle tongues wagging, rumors flying all round the place. Rumors that go on growing, and that no one can stop. Damn it all, Charles, don't you see how cruel and unnecessary it would be? You're merely indulging your vivid imagination in a gallop over a wholly speculative course."

A look of irresolution appeared on the actor's face.

"I hadn't thought of it like that," he admitted.

"You're a thundering good chap, Charles, but you do let your imagination run away with you. Come, now, do you seriously believe anyone—anyone at all—would want to murder that perfectly harmless old man?"

"I suppose not," said Sir Charles. "No, as you say, it's ridiculous. Sorry, Tollie, but it wasn't really a mere stunt on my part. I did genuinely have a hunch that something was wrong."

Mr. Satterthwaite gave a little cough.

"May I make a suggestion? Mr. Babbington was taken ill a very few moments after entering the room and just after drinking his cocktail. Now, I did happen to notice that he made a wry face when drinking. I imagined because he was unused to the taste. But supposing that Sir Bartholomew's tentative suggestion is correct—that Mr. Babbington may for some reason have wished to commit suicide. That does strike me as just possible, whereas the suggestion of murder seems quite ridiculous.

"I feel that it is possible, though not likely, that Mr. Babbington introduced something into that glass unseen by us. Now, I see that nothing has yet been touched in this room. The cocktail glasses are exactly where they were. This is Mr. Babbington's. I know because I was sitting here talking to him. I suggest that Sir Bartholomew should get the glass analyzed; that can be done quite quietly and without causing any talk."

Sir Bartholomew rose and picked up the glass.

"Right," he said. "I'll humor you so far, Charles, and I'll bet you ten pounds to one that there's nothing in it but honest-to-God gin and vermouth."

"Done," said Sir Charles. Then he added, with a rueful smile, "You know, Tollie, you are partly responsible for my flights of fancy."

"I?"

"Yes, with your talk of crime this morning. You said this man Hercule Poirot was a kind of stormy petrel, that where he went crimes followed. No sooner does he arrive than we have a suspiciously sudden death. Of course, my thoughts fly to murder at once."

"I wonder," said Mr. Satterthwaite, and stopped.

"Yes," said Charles Cartwright. "I'd thought of that. . . . What do you think, Tollie? Could we ask him what he thinks of it all? Is it etiquette, I mean?"

"A nice point," murmured Mr. Satterthwaite.

"I know medical etiquette, but I'm hanged if I know anything about the etiquette of detection."

"You can't ask a professional singer to sing," murmured Mr. Satterthwaite. "Can one ask a professional detective to detect? Yes, that is a very nice point."

"Just an opinion," said Sir Charles.

There was a gentle tap on the door and Hercule Poirot's face appeared, peering in with an apologetic expression.

"Come in, man!" cried Sir Charles, springing up. "We were just talking of you."

"I thought perhaps I might be intruding."

"Not at all. Have a drink."

"I thank you, no. I seldom drink the whisky. A glance of *sirop* now——"

But *sirop* was not included in Sir Charles's conception of drinkable fluids. Having settled his guest in a chair, the actor went straight to the point.

"I'm not going to beat about the bush," he said. "We were just talking of you, M. Poirot, and—and of what happened tonight. Look here. Do you think there's anything wrong about it?"

Poirot's eyebrows rose. He said:

"Wrong? How do you mean that—wrong?"

Bartholomew Strange said, "My friend has got an idea into his head that old Babbington was murdered."

"And you do not think so, eh?"

"We'd like to know what you think."

Poirot said thoughtfully:

"He was taken ill, of course, very suddenly—very suddenly indeed."

"Just so."

Mr. Satterthwaite explained the theory of suicide and his own suggestion of having the cocktail glass analyzed.

Poirot nodded approval.

"That, at any rate, can do no harm. As a judge of human nature, it seems to me unlikely in the extreme that anyone would wish to do away with a charming and harmless old gentleman. Still less does the solution of suicide appeal to me. However, the cocktail glass will tell us, one way or another."

"And the result of the analysis, you think, will be, what?"

Poirot shrugged his shoulders.

"Me? I can only guess. You ask me to guess what will be the result of the analysis?"

"Yes."

"Then I guess that they will find only the remains of a very excellent dry martini." He bowed to Sir Charles. "To poison a man in a cocktail—one of many handed round on a tray—well, it would be a technic very, very difficult. And if that charming old clergyman wanted to commit suicide, I do not think he would do it at a party. That would show a very decided lack of consideration for others, and Mr. Babbington struck me as a very considerate person." He paused. "That, since you ask me, is my opinion."

There was a moment's silence. Then Sir Charles gave a deep sigh. He opened one of the windows and looked out.

"Wind's gone round a point," he said.

The sailor had come back and the secret-service detective had disappeared.

But to the observant Mr. Satterthwaite it seemed as though Sir Charles hankered slightly after the part he was not, after all, to play.

CHAPTER IV

"YES, but what do you think, Mr. Satterthwaite? Really think?"

Mr. Satterthwaite looked this way and that. There was no escape. Egg Lytton Gore had got him securely cornered on the fishing quay. Merciless, these modern young women, and terrifyingly alive.

"Sir Charles has put this idea into your head," he said.

"No, he hasn't. It was there already. It's been there from the beginning. It was so frightfully sudden."

"He was an old man and his health wasn't very good——"

Egg cut the recital short:

"That's all tripe. He had neuritis and a touch of rheumatoid arthritis. That doesn't make you fall down in a fit. He never had fits. He was the sort of gentle, creaking gate that would have lived to be ninety. What did you think of the inquest?"

"It all seemed to be quite—er—normal."

"What did you think of Doctor MacDougal's evidence? Frightfully technical and all that—close description of the organs—but didn't it strike you that behind all that bombardment of words he was hedging? What he said amounted to this—that there was nothing to show that death had not arisen from natural causes. He didn't say it was the result of natural causes."

"Aren't you splitting hairs a little, my dear?"

"The point is that he did; he was puzzled, but he had *thing to go upon, so he had to take refuge in medical What did Sir Bartholomew Strange think?"

Mr. Satterthwaite repeated some of the physician's dictums.

"Pooh-poohed it, did he?" said Egg thoughtfully. "Of course, he's a cautious man; I suppose a Harley Street big bug has to be."

"There was nothing in the cocktail glass but gin and vermouth," Mr. Satterthwaite reminded her.

"That seems to settle it. All the same, something that happened after the inquest made me wonder——"

"Something he said to you?"

Mr. Satterthwaite began to feel a pleasant curiosity.

"Not to me—to Oliver—Oliver Manders; he was at dinner that night, but perhaps you don't remember him."

"Yes, I remember him very well. Is he a great friend of yours?"

"Used to be. Now we scrap most of the time. He's gone into his uncle's office in the City and he's getting—well, a bit above himself, if you know what I mean. Always talks of chucking it and being a journalist; he writes rather well. But I don't think it's any more than talk now. He wants to get rich. I think everybody is rather disgusting about money, don't you, Mr. Satterthwaite?"

Her youth came home to him then—the crude, arrogant childishness of her.

"My dear," he said, "so many people are disgusting about so many things."

"Most people are swine, of course," agreed Egg cheerfully. "That's why I'm really cut up about old Mr. Babbington. Because, you see, he really was rather a pet. He prepared me for confirmation and all that, and though, of course, a lot of that business is all bunkum, he really was rather sweet about it. You see, Mr. Satterthwaite, I really believe in Christianity—not like mother does, with little books and early service and things, but intelligently and as a matter of history. The church is all cluttered up with the Pauline tradition—in fact, the church is a mess, but Christianity, itself, is all right. That's why I can't be a Communist, like Oliver. In practice, our beliefs would work out much the same—things in common and ownership by all—but the difference—well, I needn't go into that. But the Babbingtons really were Christians; they didn't poke and pry and condemn, and they were never unkind abₒ people or things. They were pets—and there was Rob·

"Robin?"

"Their son. He was out in India and got killed. I—I had rather a pash on Robin."

Egg blinked. Her gaze went out to sea. Then her attention returned to Mr. Satterthwaite and the present.

"So, you see, I feel rather strongly about this. Supposing it wasn't a natural death."

"My dear child!"

"Well, it's damned odd! You must admit it's odd."

"But surely you yourself havé just practically admitted that the Babbingtons hadn't an enemy in the world."

"That's what's so queer about it. I can't think of any conceivable motive."

"Fantastic! There was nothing in the cocktail."

"Perhaps someone jabbed him with a hypodermic."

"Containing the arrow poison of the South American Indians," suggested Mr. Satterthwaite, gently ridiculing.

Egg grinned.

"That's it. The good old untraceable stuff. Oh, well, you're all very superior about it. Some day, perhaps, you'll find out we are right."

"We?"

"Sir Charles and I." She flushed slightly.

Mr. Satterthwaite thought in the words and meter of his generation, when *Quotations for All Occasions* was to be found in every bookcase:

> *"Of more than twice her years,*
> *Seamed with an ancient sword-cut on the cheek,*
> *And bruised and bronzed, she lifted up her eyes*
> *And loved him, with that love which was her*
> *doom."*

He felt a little ashamed of himself for thinking in quotations; Tennyson, too, was very little thought of nowadays. Besides, though Sir Charles was bronzed, he was not scarred, and Egg Lytton Gore, though doubtless capable of a healthy passion, did not look at all likely to perish of love and drift about rivers on a barge. There was nothing of the lily maid of Astolat about her.

"Except," thought Mr. Satterthwaite, "her youth."

25

Girls were always attracted to middle-aged men with interesting pasts. Egg seemed to be no exception to this rule.

"Why hasn't he ever married?" she asked abruptly.

"Well," Mr. Satterthwaite paused. His own answer, put bluntly, would have been "Caution," but he realized that such a word would be unacceptable to Egg Lytton Gore.

Sir Charles Cartwright had had plenty of affairs with women, actresses and others, but he had always managed to steer clear of matrimony. Egg was clearly seeking for a more romantic explanation.

"That girl who died of consumption—some actress, name began with an R—wasn't he supposed to be very fond of her?"

Mr. Satterthwaite remembered the lady in question. Rumor had coupled Charles Cartwright's name with hers, but only very slightly, and Mr. Satterthwaite did not for a moment believe that Sir Charles had remained unmarried in order to be faithful to her memory. He conveyed as much tactfully.

"I suppose he's had lots of affairs," said Egg.

"Er—h'm—probably," said Mr. Satterthwaite, feeling Victorian.

"I like men to have affairs," said Egg. "It shows they're not queer or anything."

Mr. Satterthwaite's Victorianism suffered a further pang. He was at a loss for a reply. Egg did not notice his discomfiture. She went on musingly:

"You know, Sir Charles is really cleverer than you'd think. He poses a lot, of course, dramatizes himself, but behind all that he's got brains. He's far better sailing a boat than you'd ever think to hear him talk. You'd think, to listen to him, that it was all pose, but it isn't. It's the same about this business. You think it's all done for effect—that he wants to play the part of the great detective. All I say is I think he'd play it rather well."

"Possibly," agreed Mr. Satterthwaite.

The inflection of his voice showed his feelings clearly enough. Egg pounced on them and expressed them in words:

"But your view is that Death of a Clergyman isn't a thriller. It's merely Regrettable Incident at a Dinner Party. Purely a social catastrophe. What did M. Poirot think? He ought to know."

"M. Poirot advised us to wait for the analysis of the cocktail, but, in his opinion, everything was quite all right."

"Oh, well," said Egg, "he's getting old. He's a back number." Mr. Satterthwaite winced. Egg went on, unconscious of brutality: "Come home and have tea with mother. She likes you. She said so."

Delicately flattered, Mr. Satterthwaite accepted the invitation.

On arrival, Egg volunteered to ring up Sir Charles and explain the non-appearance of his guest.

Mr. Satterthwaite sat down in the tiny sitting room with its faded chintzes and its well-polished pieces of furniture. It was a Victorian room, what Mr. Satterthwaite called in his own mind a lady's room, and he approved of it.

His conversation with Lady Mary was agreeable; nothing brilliant, but pleasantly chatty. They spoke of Sir Charles. Did Mr. Satterthwaite know him well? Not intimately, Mr. Satterthwaite said. He had had a financial interest in one of Sir Charles's plays some years ago. They had been friends ever since.

"He has great charm," said Lady Mary, smiling. "I feel it as well as Egg. I suppose you've discovered that Egg is suffering badly from hero worship?"

Mr. Satterthwaite wondered if, as a mother, Lady Mary was not made slightly uneasy by that hero worship. But it did not seem so.

"Egg sees so little of the world," she said, sighing. "We are so badly off. One of my cousins presented her and took her to a few things in town, but since then she has hardly been away from here, except for an occasional visit. Young people, I feel, should see plenty of people and places—especially people. Otherwise—well, propinquity is sometimes a dangerous thing."

Mr. Satterthwaite agreed, thinking of Sir Charles and the sailing, but that this was not what was in Lady Mary's mind she showed a moment or two later.

"Sir Charles's coming has done a lot for Egg. It has widened her horizon. You see, there are very few young people down here, especially men. I've always been afraid that Egg might marry someone simply from being thrown with one person only and seeing no one else."

Mr. Satterthwaite had a quick intuition.

"Are you thinking of young Oliver Manders?"

Lady Mary blushed in ingenuous surprise.

"Oh, Mr. Satterthwaite, I don't know how you knew! I was thinking of him. He and Egg were together a lot at one time, and I know I'm old-fashioned, but I don't like some of his ideas."

"Youth must have its fling," said Mr. Satterthwaite.

Lady Mary shook her head.

"I've been so afraid—— It's quite suitable, of course; I know all about him, and his uncle, who has recently taken him into his firm, is a very rich man. It's not that. It's silly of me, but——"

She shook her head, unable to express herself further.

Mr. Satterthwaite felt curiously intimate. He said quietly and plainly:

"All the same, Lady Mary, you wouldn't like your girl to marry a man twice her own age."

Her answer surprised him.

"It might be safer so. If you do that, at least you know where you are. At that age, a man's follies and sins are definitely behind him; they are not still to come."

Before Mr. Satterthwaite could say any more, Egg rejoined them.

"You've been a long time, darling," said her mother.

"I was talking to Sir Charles, my sweet. He's all alone in his glory." She turned reproachfully to Mr. Satterthwaite. "You didn't tell me the house party had flitted."

"They went back yesterday—all but Sir Bartholomew Strange. He was staying till tomorrow, but he was recalled to London by an urgent telegram this morning. One of his patients was in a critical condition."

"It's a pity," said Egg. "Because I meant to study the house party. I might have got a clue."

"A clue to what, darling?"

"Mr. Satterthwaite knows. Oh, well, it doesn't matter. Oliver's still here. We'll rope him in. He's got brains when he likes."

When Mr. Satterthwaite arrived back at Crow's Nest, he found his host sitting on the terrace overlooking the sea.

"Hullo, Satterthwaite. Been having tea with the Lytton Gores?"

28

"Yes. You didn't mind?"

"Of course not. Egg telephoned. Odd sort of girl, Egg."

"Attractive," said Mr. Satterthwaite.

"H'm, yes, I suppose she is."

He got up and walked a few aimless steps.

"I wish to God," he said suddenly and bitterly, "that I'd never come to this cursed place."

CHAPTER V

MR. Satterthwaite thought to himself, "He's got it badly."
He felt a sudden pity for his host. At the age of fifty-two,
Charles Cartwright, the gay, debonair breaker of hearts, had
fallen in love. And as he himself realized, his case was doomed
to disappointment. Youth turns to youth.

"Girls don't wear their hearts on their sleeves," thought
Mr. Satterthwaite. "Egg makes a great parade of her feeling
for Sir Charles. She wouldn't if it really meant anything.
Young Manders is the one."

Mr. Satterthwaite was usually fairly shrewd in his
assumptions.

Still, there was probably one factor that he did not take
into account, because he was unaware of it himself. That was
the enhanced value placed by age on youth. To Mr. Satterthwaite, an elderly man, the fact that Egg might prefer a
middle-aged man to a young one was frankly incredible. Youth
was to him so much the most magical of all gifts.

He felt strengthened in his beliefs when Egg rang up
after dinner and demanded permission to bring Oliver along
and "have a consultation."

Certainly a handsome lad, with his dark, heavy-lidded
eyes and easy grace of movement. He had, it seemed, permitted himself to be brought—a tribute to Egg's energy—but his
general attitude was lazily skeptical.

"Can't you talk it out of her, sir?" he said to Sir Charles.
"It's this appallingly healthy, bucolic life she leads that makes
her so energetic. . . . You know, Egg, you really are detestably
hearty. And your tastes are childish—crime, sensation, and
all that bunk."

30

"You're a skeptic, Manders?"

"Well, sir, really. That dear, old, bleating fellow. It's fantastic to think of anything else but natural causes."

"I expect you're right," said Sir Charles.

Mr. Satterthwaite glanced at him. What part was Charles Cartwright playing tonight? Not the ex-naval man, not the international detective. No, some new and unfamiliar rôle.

It came as a shock to Mr. Satterthwaite when he realized what that rôle was. Sir Charles was playing second fiddle. Second fiddle to Oliver Manders.

He sat back with his head in shadow, watching those two, Egg and Oliver, as they disputed—Egg hotly, Oliver languidly. Sir Charles looked older than usual—old and tired.

More than once Egg appealed to him, hotly and confidently, but his response was lacking.

It was eleven o'clock when they left. Sir Charles went out on the terrace with them and offered the loan of an electric torch to help them down the stony path.

But there was no need of a torch. It was a beautiful moonlit night. They set off together, their voices growing fainter as they descended.

Moonlight or no moonlight, Mr. Satterthwaite was not going to risk a chill. He returned to the ship room. Sir Charles stayed out on the terrace a little while longer.

When he came in, he latched the window behind him, and striding to a side table, poured himself out a whisky and soda.

"Satterthwaite," he said, "I'm leaving here tomorrow for good."

"What?" cried Mr. Satterthwaite, astonished.

A kind of melancholy pleasure at the effect he had produced showed for a minute on Charles Cartwright's face.

"It's the Only Thing to Do," he said, obviously speaking in capital letters. "I shall sell this place. What it has meant to me, no one will ever know." His voice dropped, lingeringly, effectively.

After an evening of second fiddle, Sir Charles's egoism was taking its revenge.

This was the great renunciation scene, so often played by him in sundry and divers dramas. Giving up the other man's wife; renouncing the girl he loved.

31

There was a brave flippancy in his voice as he went on: "Cut your losses; it's the only way. Youth to youth. They're made for each other, those two. I shall clear out."

"Where to?" asked Mr. Satterthwaite.

The actor made a careless gesture.

"Anywhere. What does it matter?" He added, with a slight change of voice, "Probably Monte Carlo." And then, retrieving what his sensitive taste could not but feel to be a slight anticlimax, "In the heart of the desert or the heart of the crowd, what does it matter? The inmost core of man is solitary, alone. I have always been a lonely soul."

It was clearly an exit line.

He nodded to Mr. Satterthwaite and left the room.

Mr. Satterthwaite got up and prepared to follow his host to bed.

"But it won't be the heart of a desert," he thought to himself, with a slight chuckle.

On the following morning, Sir Charles begged Mr. Satterthwaite to forgive him if he went up to town that day.

"Don't cut your visit short, my dear fellow. You were staying till tomorrow, and I know you're going on to the Harbertons' at Tavistock. The car will take you there. What I feel is that having come to my decision, I mustn't look back. No, I mustn't look back."

Sir Charles squared his shoulders with manly resolution, wrung Mr. Satterthwaite's hand with fervor and delivered him over to the capable Miss Milray.

Miss Milray seemed prepared to deal with the situation as she had dealt with any other. She expressed no surprise or emotion at Sir Charles's overnight decision. Nor could Mr. Satterthwaite draw her out on the point. Neither sudden deaths nor sudden changes of plan could excite Miss Milray. She accepted whatever happened as a fact and proceeded to cope with it in an efficient way. She telephoned to the house agents, dispatched wires abroad, and wrote busily on her typewriter. Mr. Satterthwaite escaped from the depressing spectacle of so much efficiency by strolling down to the quay. He was walking aimlessly along when he was seized by the arm from behind and turned to confront a white-faced girl.

"What's all this?" demanded Egg fiercely.

"All what?" parried Mr. Satterthwaite.

"It's all over the place that Sir Charles is going away— that he's going to sell Crow's Nest."

"Quite true."

"He is going away?"

"He's gone."

"Oh!" Egg relinquished his arm. She looked suddenly like a very small child who has been cruelly hurt.

Mr. Satterthwaite did not know what to say.

"Where has he gone?"

"Abroad. To the South of France."

"Oh!"

Still he did not know what to say. For clearly there was more than hero worship here.

Pitying her, he was turning over various consolatory words in his mind, when she spoke again, and startled him.

"Which of those damned women is it?" asked Egg fiercely.

Mr. Satterthwaite stared at her, his mouth fallen open in surprise. Egg took him by the arm again and shook him violently.

"You must know!" she cried. "Which of them? The gray-haired one or the other?"

"My dear, I don't know what you're talking about."

"You do! You must! Of course, it's some woman. He liked me—I know he liked me. One of those two women the other night must have seen it, too, and determined to get him away from me. I hate women. Lousy cats. Did you see her clothes— that one with the green hair? They made me gnash my teeth with envy. A woman who has clothes like that has a pull— you can't deny it. She's quite old and ugly as sin, really, but what does it matter? She makes everyone else look like a dowdy curate's wife. Is it her? Or is it the other one with the gray hair? She's amusing—you can see that. She's got masses of S. A. And he called her Angie. It can't be the one like a wilted cabbage. Is it the smart one or is it Angie?"

"My dear, you've got the most extraordinary ideas into your head. He—er—Charles Cartwright isn't in the least interested in either of those women."

"I don't believe you. They're interested in him anyway."

"No, no, no, you're making a mistake. This is all imagination. I can assure you that you are laboring under a misapprehension."

33

"Then why has he gone away like this?"

Mr. Satterthwaite cleared his throat.

"I fancy he—er—thought it best."

Egg stared at him piercingly.

"Do you mean because of me?"

"Well, something of the kind, perhaps."

"And so he's legged it. I suppose I did show my hand a bit plainly. Men do hate being chased, don't they? Mums is right, after all. You've no idea how sweet she is when she talks about men. Always in the third person—so Victorian and polite. 'A man hates being run after'; 'a girl should always let the man make the running.' Don't you think it's a sweet expression—'make the running'? Sounds the opposite of what it means. Actually, that's just what Charles has done—made the running. He's run away from me. He's afraid. And the devil of it is I can't go after him. If I did, I suppose he'd take a boat to the wilds of Africa or somewhere."

"Hermione," said Mr. Satterthwaite, "are you serious about Sir Charles?"

The girl flung him an impatient glance.

"Of course I am."

"What about Oliver Manders?"

Egg dismissed Oliver Manders with an impatient whisk of the head. She was following out a train of thought of her own.

"Do you think that I might write to him? Nothing alarming. Just chatty, girlish stuff. You know, put him at his ease, so that he'd get over his scare."

She frowned.

"What a fool I've been. Mums would have managed it much better. They knew how to do the trick, those Victorians. All blushing retreat. I've been all wrong about it. I actually thought he needed encouraging. He seemed—well, he seemed to need a bit of help. Tell me"—she turned abruptly on Mr. Satterthwaite—"did he see me do my kissing act with Oliver last night?"

"Not that I know of. When?"

"All in the moonlight. As we were going down the path. I thought he was still looking from the terrace. I thought perhaps if he saw me and Oliver—well, I thought it might wake him up a bit. Because he did like me. I could swear he liked me."

"Wasn't that a little hard on Oliver?"

Egg shook her head decisively.

"Not in the least. Oliver thinks it's an honor for any girl to be kissed by him. It was bad for his conceit, of course, but one can't think of everything. I wanted to ginger up Charles. He's been different lately—more standoffish."

"My dear child," said Mr. Satterthwaite, "I don't think you realize quite why Sir Charles went away so suddenly. He thought that you cared for Oliver. He went away to save himself further pain."

Egg whisked round. She caught hold of Mr. Satterthwaite by the shoulders and peered into his face.

"Is that true? Is that really true? The mutt! The boob! Oh!"

She released Mr. Satterthwaite suddenly and moved along beside him with a skipping motion.

"Then he'll come back," she said. "He'll come back. If he doesn't——"

"Well, if he doesn't?"

Egg laughed.

"I'll get him back somehow. You see if I don't."

It seemed as though, allowing for difference of language, Egg and the lily maid of Astolat had much in common, but Mr. Satterthwaite felt that Egg's methods would be more practical than those of Elaine, and that dying of a broken heart would form no part of them.

SECOND ACT

CERTAINTY

CHAPTER VI

MR. Satterthwaite had come over for the day to Monte
Carlo. His round of house parties was over, and the Riviera in
September was rather a favorite haunt of his.

He was sitting in the gardens enjoying the sun and reading a two-days-old *Daily Mail.*

Suddenly a name caught his attention: "Strange." "Death
of Sir Bartholomew Strange." He read the paragraph through:

> We much regret having to announce the death
> of Sir Bartholomew Strange, the eminent nerve spe-
> cialist. Sir Bartholomew was entertaining a party
> of friends at his house in Yorkshire. Sir Bartholomew
> appeared to be in perfect health and spirits, and
> his demise occurred quite suddenly at the end of
> dinner. He was chatting with his friends and drink-
> ing a glass of port when he had a sudden seizure
> and died before medical aid could be summoned.
> Sir Bartholomew will be deeply regretted.
>
> He was——

Here followed a description of Sir Bartholomew's career
and work.

Mr. Satterthwaite let the paper slip from his hand. He
was very disagreeably impressed. A vision of the physician as
he had seen him last flashed across his mind—big, jocund, in
the pink of condition. And now dead. Certain words detached
themselves from their context and floated about disagreeably
in Mr. Satterthwaite's mind. "Drinking a glass of port . . .

sudden seizure ... died before medical aid could be summoned. ..."

Port, not a cocktail, but otherwise curiously reminiscent of that death in Cornwall. Mr. Satterthwaite saw again the convulsed face of the mild old clergyman.

Supposing that, after all——

He looked up to see Sir Charles Cartwright coming toward him across the grass.

"Satterthwaite, by all that's wonderful! Just the man I'd have chosen to see. Have you seen about poor old Tollie?"

"I was just reading it now."

Sir Charles dropped into a chair beside him. He was immaculately got up in yachting costume. No more gray flannels and old sweaters. He was the sophisticated yachtsman of the South of France.

"Listen, Satterthwaite; Tollie was as sound as a bell. Never had anything wrong with him. Am I being a complete fanciful ass, or does this business remind you of—of——"

"Of that business at Loomouth? Yes, it does. But of course we may be mistaken. The resemblance may be only superficial. After all, sudden deaths occur the whole time from a variety of causes."

Sir Charles nodded his head impatiently. Then he said:

"I've just got a letter from Egg Lytton Gore."

Mr. Satterthwaite concealed a smile.

"The first you've had from her?"

Sir Charles was unsuspecting:

"No, I had a letter soon after I got here. It followed me about a bit. Just giving me the news and all that. I didn't answer it. . . . Dash it all, Satterthwaite, I didn't dare answer it. The girl had no idea, of course, but I didn't want to make a fool of myself."

Mr. Satterthwaite passed his hand over his mouth, where the smile still lingered.

"And this one?" he asked.

"This is different. It's an appeal for help."

"An appeal for help?" Mr. Satterthwaite's eyebrows went up.

"She was there, you see—in the house—when it happened."

"You mean she was staying with Sir Bartholomew Strange at the time of his death?"

"Yes."

"What does she say about it?"

Sir Charles had taken a letter from his pocket. He hesitated for a moment, then he handed it to Mr. Satterthwaite.

"You'd better read it for yourself."

Mr. Satterthwaite opened out the sheet with lively curiosity.

> *Dear Sir Charles:* I don't know when this will get to you. I do hope soon. I'm so worried I don't know what to do. You'll have seen, I expect, in the papers that Sir Bartholomew Strange is dead. Well, he died just the same way as Mr. Babbington. It can't be a coincidence—it can't—it can't. . . . I'm worried to death.
>
> Look here; can't you come home and do something? It sounds a bit crude put like that, but you did have suspicions before and nobody would listen to you, and now it's your own friend who's been killed, and perhaps, if you don't come back, nobody will ever find out the truth, and I'm sure you could. I feel it in my bones.
>
> And there's something else. I'm worried, definitely, about someone. He had absolutely nothing to do with it, I know that, but things might look a bit odd. Oh, I can't explain in a letter, but won't you come back? You could find out the truth. I know you could.
>
> Yours in haste,
> EGG.

"Well?" demanded Sir Charles impatiently. "A bit incoherent, of course; she wrote it in a hurry. But what about it?"

Mr. Satterthwaite folded the letter slowly to give himself a minute or two before replying.

He agreed that the letter was incoherent, but he did not think it had been written in a hurry. It was, in his view, a very careful production. It was designed to appeal to Sir Charles's vanity, to his chivalry, and to his sporting instinct.

41

From what Mr. Satterthwaite knew of Sir Charles, that letter was a certain draw.

"Who do you think she means by 'someone,' and 'he'?" he asked.

"Manders, I suppose."

"Was he there, then?"

"Must have been. I don't know why. Tollie never met him except on that one occasion at my house. Why he should ask him to stay, I can't imagine."

"Did he often have those big house parties?"

"Three or four times a year. Always one for the St. Leger."

"Did he spend much time in Yorkshire?"

"Had a big sanatorium, nursing home, whatever you like to call it. He bought Melfort Abbey—it's an old place—restored it and built a sanatorium in the grounds."

"I see."

Mr. Satterthwaite was silent for a minute or two. Then he said:

"I wonder who else there was in the house party?"

Sir Charles suggested that it might be in one of the other newspapers, and they went off to institute a newspaper hunt.

"Here we are," said Sir Charles.

He read aloud:

" 'Sir Bartholomew Strange is having his usual house party for the St. Leger. Amongst the guests are Lord and Lady Eden, Lady Mary and Miss Hermione Lytton Gore, Sir Jocelyn and Lady Cambell, Captain and Mrs. Dacres, and Miss Angela Sutcliffe, the well-known actress.' "

Sir Charles and Mr. Satterthwaite looked at each other.

"The Dacreses and Angela Sutcliffe," said Sir Charles. "Nothing about Oliver Manders."

"Let's get today's *Continental Daily Mail*," said Mr. Satterthwaite. "There might be something in that."

Sir Charles glanced over the paper. Suddenly he stiffened.

"Listen to this, Satterthwaite:

" 'Death of Sir Bartholomew Strange. At the

inquest today on the late Sir Bartholomew Strange, a verdict of death by nicotine poisoning was returned; there being no evidence to show how or by whom the poison was administered.' "

He frowned.

"Nicotine poisoning. Sounds mild enough—not the sort of thing to make a man fall down in a fit. I don't understand all this."

"What are you going to do?"

"Do? I'm going to book a berth on the Blue Train tonight."

"Well," said Mr. Satterthwaite, "I might as well do the same."

"You?" Sir Charles wheeled round on him, surprised.

"This sort of thing is rather in my line," said Mr. Satterthwaite modestly. "I've—er—had a little experience. Besides, I know the chief constable in that part of the world rather well—Colonel Johnson. That will come in useful."

"Good man!" cried Sir Charles. "Let's go round to the Wagons-Lits offices."

Mr. Satterthwaite thought to himself:

"The girl's done it. She's got him back. She said she would. I wonder just exactly how much of her letter was genuine."

Decidedly, Egg Lytton Gore was an opportunist.

When Sir Charles had gone off to the Wagons-Lits offices, Mr. Satterthwaite strolled slowly through the gardens. His mind was still pleasantly engaged with the problem of Egg Lytton Gore. He admired her resource and her driving power, and stifled that slight Victorian side of his nature which disapproved of a member of the fairer sex taking the initiative in affairs of the heart.

Mr. Satterthwaite was an observant man. In the midst of his cogitations on the female sex in general and Egg Lytton Gore in particular, he was unable to resist saying to himself:

"Now where have I seen that particular-shaped head before?"

The owner of the head was sitting on a seat gazing thoughtfully ahead of him. He was a little man whose mustaches were out of proportion to his size.

A discontented-looking English child was standing nearby, standing first on one foot, then the other, and occasionally meditatively kicking the lobelia edging.

"Don't do that, darling," said her mother, who was absorbed in a fashion paper.

"I haven't anything to do," said the child.

The little man turned his head to look at her, and Mr. Satterthwaite recognized him.

"M. Poirot," he said, "this is a very pleasant surprise."

M. Poirot rose and bowed.

"Enchanté, monsieur."

They shook hands and Mr. Satterthwaite sat down.

"Everyone seems to be in Monte Carlo. Not half an hour ago I ran across Sir Charles Cartwright, and now you."

"Sir Charles, he also is here?"

"He's been yachting. You know that he gave up his house at Loomouth?"

"Ah, no, I did not know it. I am surprised."

"I don't know that I am. He worked too hard at his own profession; had a bit of a breakdown and had to retire; but I don't think Cartwright is really the kind of man who likes to live permanently out of the world."

"Ah, no, I agree with you there. I was surprised for another reason. It seemed to me that Sir Charles had a particular reason for staying in Loomouth—a very charming reason. Eh, am I not right? The little *demoiselle* who calls herself, so amusingly, the egg?"

His eyes were twinkling gently.

"Oh, so you noticed that?"

"Assuredly I noticed. I have the heart very susceptible to lovers—you, too, I think. And *la jeunesse,* it is always touching."

He sighed.

"I think," said Mr. Satterthwaite, "that actually you have hit on Sir Charles's reason for leaving Loomouth. He was running away."

"From Mademoiselle Egg? But it is obvious that she adores him. Why, then, run?"

"Ah," said Mr. Satterthwaite. "You don't understand our Anglo-Saxon complexes."

M. Poirot was following his own line of reasoning.

"Of course," he said. "It is a good move to pursue. Run

44

from a woman; immediately she follows. Doubtless Sir Charles, a man of much experience, knows that."

Mr. Satterthwaite was rather amused.

"I don't think it was quite that way," he said. "Tell me, what are you doing out here? A holiday?"

"My time is all holidays nowadays. I have succeeded. I am rich. I retire. Now I travel about, seeing the world."

"Splendid," said Mr. Satterthwaite.

"*N'est-ce pas?*"

"Mummy," said the English child, "isn't there anything to do?"

"Darling," said her mother reproachfully, "isn't it lovely to have come abroad and to be in the beautiful sunshine?"

"Yes, but there's nothing to do."

"Run about, amuse yourself. Go and look at the sea."

"*Maman,*" said a French child, suddenly appearing, "*joue avec moi.*"

A French mother looked up from her book.

"*Amuse-toi avec ta balle, Marcelle.*"

Obediently the French child bounced her ball with a gloomy face.

"*Je m'amuse,*" said Hercule Poirot, and there was a very curious expression on his face.

Then, as if in answer to something he read in Mr. Satterthwaite's face, he said:

"But yes, you have the quick perceptions. It is as you think."

He was silent for a minute or two, then he said:

"See you, as a boy I was poor. There were many of us. We had to get on in the world. I entered the police force. I worked hard. Slowly I rose in that force. I began to make a name for myself. I made a name for myself. I began to acquire an international reputation. At last I was due to retire. There came the war. I was injured. I came, a sad and weary refugee, to England. A kind lady gave me hospitality. She died; not naturally; no, she was killed. *Eh bien,* I set my wits to work. I employed my little gray cells. I discovered her murderer. I found that I was not yet finished. No, indeed, my powers were stronger than ever. Then began my second career—that of a private inquiry agent in England. I have solved many fascinating and baffling problems. Ah, monsieur, I have lived!"

45

The psychology of human nature, it is wonderful. I grew rich. 'Some day,' I said to myself, 'I will have all the money I need. I will realize all my dreams.' "

He laid a hand on Mr. Satterthwaite's knee.

"My friend, beware of the day when your dreams come true. That child near us, doubtless she, too, has dreamed of coming abroad—of the excitement—of how different everything would be. You understand?"

"I understand," said Mr. Satterthwaite, "that you are not amusing yourself."

Poirot nodded.

"Exactly."

There were moments when Mr. Satterthwaite looked like Puck. This was one of them. His little wrinkled face twitched impishly. He hesitated. Should he? Should he not?

Slowly he unfolded the newspaper he was still carrying. "Have you seen this, M. Poirot?"

With his forefinger he indicated the paragraph he meant.

The little Belgian took the paper. Mr. Satterthwaite watched him as he read. No change came over his face, but the Englishman had the impression that his body stiffened, as does that of a terrier when it sniffs a rat hole.

Hercule Poirot read the paragraph twice, then he folded the paper and returned it to Mr. Satterthwaite.

"That is interesting," he said.

"Yes. It looks, does it not, as though Sir Charles Cartwright had been right and we had been wrong?"

"Yes," said Poirot. "It seems as though we had been wrong. I will admit it, my friend. I could not believe that so harmless, so friendly an old man could have been murdered. Well, it may be that I was wrong. Although, you see, this other death may be coincidence. Coincidences do occur—the most amazing coincidences. I know; I, Hercule Poirot, have known coincidences that surprise you."

He paused and went on:

"Sir Charles Cartwright's instinct may have been right. He is an artist—sensitive, impressionable. He feels things rather than reasons about them. Such a method in life is often disastrous, but it is sometimes justified. I wonder where Sir Charles is now."

Mr. Satterthwaite smiled.

"I can tell you that. He is in the office of the Wagons-Lits Company. He and I are returning to England tonight."

"Aha!" Poirot put immense meaning into the exclamation. His eyes, bright, inquiring, roguish, asked a question: "What zeal he has, our Sir Charles. He is determined, then, to play this rôle—the rôle of the amateur policeman? Or is there another reason?"

Mr. Satterthwaite did not reply, but from his silence Poirot seemed to deduce an answer.

"I see," he said. "The bright eyes of mademoiselle are concerned in this. It is not only crime that calls?"

"She wrote to him," said Mr. Satterthwaite, "begging him to return."

Poirot nodded.

"I wonder now," he said. "I do not quite understand——"

Mr. Satterthwaite interrupted:

"You do not understand the modern English girl? Well, that is not surprising. I do not always understand them myself. A girl like Miss Lytton Gore——"

In his turn, Poirot interrupted:

"Pardon. You have misunderstood me. I understand Miss Lytton Gore very well. I have met such another—many such others. You call the type modern, but it is—how shall I say? —age long."

Mr. Satterthwaite was slightly annoyed. He felt that he, and only he, understood Egg. This preposterous foreigner knew nothing about young English womanhood.

Poirot was still speaking. His tone was dreamy, brooding:

"A knowledge of human nature—what a dangerous thing it can be."

"A useful thing," corrected Mr. Satterthwaite.

"Perhaps. It depends upon the point of view."

"Well——" Mr. Satterthwaite hesitated, got up. He was a little disappointed. He had cast the bait and the fish had not risen. He felt that his own knowledge of human nature was at fault. "I will wish you a pleasant holiday."

"I thank you."

"I hope that, when you are next in London, you will come and see me." He produced a card. "This is my address."

"You are most amiable, Mr. Satterthwaite. I shall be charmed."

47

"Good-bye for the present, then."

"Good-bye and bon voyage."

Mr. Satterthwaite moved away. Poirot looked after him for a moment or two, then once more he stared straight ahead of him, looking out over the blue Mediterranean.

So he sat for at least ten minutes.

The English child reappeared.

"I've looked at the sea, mummy. What shall I do next?"

"An admirable question," said Hercule Poirot under his breath.

He rose and walked slowly away—in the direction of the Wagons-Lits offices.

CHAPTER VII

SIR Charles and Mr. Satterthwaite were sitting in Colonel Johnson's study. The chief constable was a big, red-faced man with a barrack-room voice and a hearty manner.

He had greeted Mr. Satterthwaite with every sign of pleasure and was obviously delighted to make the acquaintance of the famous Charles Cartwright.

"My missus is a great playgoer. She's one of your—what do the Americans call it?—fans. That's it—fans. I like a good play myself—good clean stuff, that is. Some of the things they put on the stage nowadays—faugh!"

Sir Charles, conscious of rectitude in this respect—he had never put on daring plays—responded suitably with all his easy charm of manner. When they came to mention the object of their visit, Colonel Johnson was only too ready to tell them all he could.

"Friend of yours, you say? Too bad—too bad. Yes, he was very popular around here. That sanatorium of his is very highly spoken of, and, by all accounts, Sir Bartholomew was a first-rate fellow as well as being at the top of his profession. Kind, generous, popular all round. Last man in the world you'd expect to be murdered—and murder is what it looks like. There's nothing to indicate suicide, and anything like accident seems out of the question."

"Satterthwaite and I have just come back from abroad," said Sir Charles. "We've only seen snippets here and there in the papers."

"And, naturally, you want to know all about it. Well, I'll tell you exactly how the matter stands. I think there's no doubt the butler's the man we've got to look for. He was a new man. Sir Bartholomew had only had him a fortnight, and the moment after the crime he disappears—vanishes into thin air. That looks a bit fishy, doesn't it? Eh, what?"

"You've no notion where he went?"

Colonel Johnson's naturally red face got a little redder.

"Negligence on our part, you think. I admit it looks like it. Naturally the fellow was under observation, just the same as everyone else. He answered our questions quite satisfactorily—gave the London agency which obtained him the place. Last employer, Sir Horace Bird. All very civil-spoken, no signs of panic. Next thing was he'd gone, and the house under observation. I've hauled my men over the coals, but they swear they didn't bat an eyelid."

"Very remarkable," said Mr. Satterthwaite.

"Apart from everything else," said Sir Charles thoughtfully, "it seems a damn-fool thing to do. As far as he knew, the man wasn't suspected. By bolting, he draws attention to himself."

"Exactly. And not a hope of escape. His description's been circulated. It's only a matter of days before he's pulled in."

"Very odd," said Sir Charles. "I don't understand it."

"Oh, the reason's clear enough. He lost his nerve. Got the wind up suddenly."

"Wouldn't a man who had the nerve to commit murder have the nerve to sit still afterwards?"

"Depends. Depends. I know criminals. Chicken-livered, most of them. He thought he was suspected and he bolted."

"Have you verified his own account of himself?"

"Naturally, Sir Charles. That's plain routine work. London agency confirms his story. He had a written reference from Sir Horace Bird, recommending him warmly. Sir Horace himself is in West Africa."

"So the reference might have been forged?"

"Exactly," said Colonel Johnson, beaming upon Sir Charles with the air of a schoolmaster congratulating a bright pupil. "We've wired to Sir Horace, of course, but it may be some little time before we get a reply. He's on *safari*."

"When did the man disappear?"

"Morning after the death. There was a doctor present at

50

the dinner—Sir Jocelyn Cambell—bit of a toxicologist, I understand. He and Davis—local man—agreed over the case, and our people were called in immediately. We interviewed everybody that night. Ellis—that's the butler—went to his room that night and was missing in the morning. His bed hadn't been slept in."

"He slipped away under cover of the darkness?"

"Seems so. One of the ladies staying there—Miss Sutcliffe, the actress—— You know her, perhaps?"

"Very well indeed."

"Miss Sutcliffe has made a suggestion to us. She suggested that the man had left the house through a secret passage." He blew his nose apologetically. "Sounds rather Edgar Wallace stuff, but it seems there was such a thing. Sir Bartholomew was rather proud of it. He showed it to Miss Sutcliffe. The end of it comes out among some fallen masonry about half a mile away."

"That would be a possible explanation, certainly," agreed Sir Charles. "Only, would the butler know of the existence of such a passage?"

"That's the point, of course. My missus always says servants know everything. Dare say she's right."

"I understand the poison was nicotine," said Mr. Satterthwaite.

"That's right. Most unusual stuff to use, I believe. Comparatively rare. I understand if a man's a heavy smoker, such as the doctor was, it would tend to complicate matters. I mean he might have died of nicotine poisoning in a natural way. Only, of course, this business was too sudden for that."

"How was it administered?"

"We don't know," admitted Colonel Johnson. "That's going to be the weak part of the case. According to medical evidence, it could only have been swallowed a few minutes previous to death."

"They were drinking port, I understand?"

"Exactly. Seems as though the stuff was in the port. But it wasn't. We analyzed his glass. That glass had contained port and nothing but port. The other wineglasses had been cleared, of course, but they were all on a tray in the pantry, unwashed, and not one of them contained anything it shouldn't. As for what he ate, it was the same as everybody else had.

51

Soup, grilled sole, pheasant and chipped potatoes, chocolate *soufflé*, soft roes on toast. His cook's been with him fifteen years. No, there doesn't seem to be any way he could have been given the stuff, and yet there it is in the stomach. It's a nasty problem."

Sir Charles wheeled round on Mr. Satterthwaite.

"The same thing," he said excitedly. "Exactly the same as before."

He turned apologetically to the chief constable.

"I must explain. A death occurred at my house in Cornwall——"

Colonel Johnson looked interested.

"I think I've heard about that. From a young lady—Miss Lytton Gore."

"Yes, she was there. She told you about it?"

"She did. She was very set on her theory. But you know, Sir Charles, I can't believe there's anything in that theory. It doesn't explain the flight of the butler. Your man didn't disappear, by any chance?"

"Haven't got a man; only a parlormaid."

"She couldn't have been a man in disguise?"

Thinking of the smart and obviously feminine Temple, Sir Charles smiled.

Colonel Johnson also smiled apologetically.

"Just an idea," he said. "No, I can't say I put much reliance in Miss Lytton Gore's theory. I understand that the death in question was an elderly clergyman. Who would want to put an old clergyman out of the way?"

"That's just the puzzling part of it," said Sir Charles.

"I think you'll find it's just coincidence. Depend on it, the butler's our man. Very likely he's a regular criminal. Unluckily, we can't find any of his fingerprints. We had a fingerprint expert go over his bedroom and the butler's pantry, but he had no luck."

"If it was the butler, what motive can you suggest?"

"That, of course, is one of our difficulties," admitted Colonel Johnson. "The man might have been there with intent to steal, and Sir Bartholomew might have caught him out."

Both Sir Charles and Mr. Satterthwaite remained courteously silent. Colonel Johnson himself seemed to feel that the suggestion lacked plausibility.

"The fact of the matter is, one can only theorize. Once we've got John Ellis under lock and key and have found out who he is and whether he's ever been through our hands before—well, the motive may be clear as day."

"You've been through Sir Bartholomew's papers, I suppose?"

"Naturally, Sir Charles. We've given that side of the case every attention. I must introduce you to Superintendent Crossfield, who has charge of the case. A most reliable man. I pointed out to him, and he was quick to agree with me, that Sir Bartholomew's profession might have had something to do with the crime. A doctor knows many professional secrets. Sir Bartholomew's papers were all neatly filed and docketed; his secretary, Miss Lyndon, went through them with Crossfield."

"And there was nothing?"

"Nothing at all suggestive, Sir Charles."

"Was anything missing from the house—silver, jewelry—anything like that?"

"Nothing whatsoever."

"Who exactly was staying in the house?"

"I've got a list. . . . Now where is it? Ah, I think Crossfield has it. You must meet Crossfield. As a matter of fact, I'm expecting him any minute now to report——" As a bell went: "That's probably the man now."

Superintendent Crossfield was a large, solid-looking man, rather slow of speech, but with a fairly keen blue eye.

He saluted his superior officer and was introduced to the two visitors.

It is possible that had Mr. Satterthwaite been alone, he would have found it hard to make Crossfield unbend. Crossfield didn't hold with gentlemen from London, amateurs, coming down with "ideas." Sir Charles, however, was a different matter. Superintendent Crossfield had a childish reverence for the glamour of the stage. He had twice seen Sir Charles act, and the excitement and rapture of seeing this hero of the footlights in a flesh-and-blood manner made him as friendly and loquacious as could be wished.

"I saw you in London, sir, I did. I was up with the wife. *Lord Aintree's Dilemma*—that's what the play was. In the pit I was, and the house crowded out; we had to stand two hours beforehand. But nothing else would do for the wife. 'I must

53

see Sir Charles Cartwright in 'Lord Aintree's Dilemma,' she said. At the Pall Mall Theater it was."

"Well," said Sir Charles, "I've retired from the stage now, as you know. Worked too hard and had a bad breakdown two years ago. But they still know my name at the Pall Mall." He took out a card and wrote a few words on it. "You give this to the people at the box office the next time you and Mrs. Crossfield are having a jaunt to town, and they'll give you a couple of the best seats going."

"I take that very kindly of you, Sir Charles—very kindly indeed. My wife will be all worked up when I tell her about this."

After this, Superintendent Crossfield was as wax in the ex-actor's hands.

"It's an odd case, sir. Never came across a case of nicotine poisoning before in all my experience. No more than our Doctor Davis."

"I always thought it was a kind of disease you got from oversmoking."

"To tell the truth, so did I, sir. But the doctor says that the pure alkaloid is an odorless liquid and that a few drops of it are enough to kill a man almost instantaneously."

Sir Charles whistled.

"Potent stuff."

"As you say, sir. And yet it's in common use, as you might say. Solutions are used to spray roses with. And of course it can be extracted from ordinary tobacco."

"Roses," said Sir Charles. "Now where have I heard——"

He frowned, then shook his head.

"Anything fresh to report, Crossfield?" asked Colonel Johnson.

"Nothing definite, sir. We've had reports that our man, Ellis, has been seen at Durham, at Ipswich, at Balham, at Land's End and a dozen other places. That's all got to be sifted out for what it's worth." He turned to the other two. "The moment a man's description is circulated as wanted, he's seen by someone all over England."

"What is the man's description?" asked Sir Charles.

Johnson took up a paper.

"John Ellis, medium height, say five foot seven or eight, stoops slightly, gray hair, small side whiskers, dark eyes,

54

husky voice, tooth missing in upper jaw visible when he smiles, no special marks or characteristics."

"H'm," said Sir Charles. "Very nondescript, bar the side whiskers and the tooth, and the first will be off by now, and you can't rely on his smiling."

"The trouble is," said Crossfield, "that nobody observes anything. The difficulty I had in getting anything but the vaguest description out of the maids at the abbey. It's always the same. I've had descriptions of one and the same man, and he's been called tall, thin, short, stout, medium height, thick-set, slender. Not one in fifty really uses his eyes properly."

"You're satisfied in your own mind, superintendent, that Ellis is the man?"

"Why else did he bolt, sir? You can't get away from that."

"That's the stumbling block," said Sir Charles thoughtfully.

Mr. Satterthwaite repeated Sir Charles's former question as to Bartholomew Strange's papers.

"Couldn't find anything there, sir. Everything seemed perfectly straight and aboveboard."

"That's so," put in Johnson. "I had a look at them myself. There was nothing in the least out of the way."

"I remember seeing Tollie's secretary once, I think," said Sir Charles. "Efficient sort of girl, but rather plain."

"That's right, sir. A very nice young lady, though, and most businesslike. By the way, we went through Sir Bartholomew's diary. Just a notebook really—that's all it is. I've got it here."

"Oh." Sir Charles held out an eager hand.

The superintendent handed him a little green book, rather shabby and worn.

Mr. Satterthwaite looked over Sir Charles's shoulder as the latter turned the leaves.

The entries were mere pencil jottings:

Old Lathom's sale. Some good port. Must remember to go.

Tell L to get new set table mats.

Feeling all in. Shall retire soon.

Note—blow up that damn fool gardener. Why can't he plant the tulips thick enough?

The last entry was dated the day before the tragedy. It ran as follows:

> Am worried about M——. Don't like the look of things.
> Tell L springs of sofa gone.

"L is Miss Lyndon," explained the superintendent.
"And M?"
"We don't know. Possibly one of his patients."
Sir Charles then asked for the list of inmates of the abbey on the night of the crime. It ran as follows:

> Martha Leckie, cook.
> Beatrice Church, upper housemaid.
> Doris Coker, under housemaid.
> Victoria Ball, parlormaid.
> Violet Bassington, kitchenmaid.

> Above have all been in the service of deceased for some time and bear good characters. Mrs. Leckie has been there for fifteen years.

> Gladys Lyndon, secretary, thirty-three, has been secretary to Sir Bartholomew Strange for three years; can give no information as to likely motive.

> Guests:
> Lord and Lady Eden, Cadogan Square, London.
> Sir Jocelyn and Lady Cambell, Harley Street, London.
> Miss Angela Sutcliffe, Cantrell Mansions, London, S.W. 3.
> Captain and Mrs. Dacres, St. John's House, London, W. 1. Mrs. Dacres carries on business as Ambrosine, Ltd., Bruton Street, London.
> Lady Mary and Miss Hermione Lytton Gore, Rose Cottage, Loomouth.
> Miss Muriel Wills, Upper Cathcart Road, Tooting.

Mr. Oliver Manders, Messrs. Speier & Ross,
Old Broad Street, E.C.

"H'm," said Sir Charles, "the Tooting touch is omitted
by the papers. I see young Manders was here too."

"That's by way of being an accident, sir," said Superintendent Crossfield. "The young gentleman ran his motorcycle
into a wall just by the abbey, and Sir Bartholomew, who, I
understand, was slightly acquainted with him, asked him to
stay the night."

"Careless thing to do," said Sir Charles cheerfully.

"It was that, sir," said the superintendent. "In fact, I
fancy myself that the young gentleman must have had one
over the eight, as the saying goes. What made him ram the wall
just where he did, I can't imagine, if he was sober at the
time."

"Just high spirit, I expect," said Sir Charles.

"Spirits, it was, in my opinion, sir."

"Well, thank you very much, superintendent. . . . Any
objection to our going and having a look at the abbey, Colonel
Johnson?"

"Of course not, my dear sir. Though I'm afraid you won't
learn much more there than I can tell you."

"Anybody there?"

"Only the domestic staff, sir. The house party left immediately after the inquest, and Miss Lyndon has returned to
Harley Street."

"We might, perhaps, see Doctor—er—Davis too?" suggested Mr. Satterthwaite.

"Good idea."

They obtained the doctor's address, and having thanked
Colonel Johnson warmly for his kindness, they left.

CHAPTER VIII

As they walked along the street, Sir Charles said:

"Any ideas, Satterthwaite?"

"What about you?" asked Mr. Satterthwaite. He liked to reserve judgment until the last possible moment.

Not so Sir Charles; he spoke emphatically:

"They're wrong, Satterthwaite. They're all wrong. They've got the butler on the brain. The butler's done a bunk—*ergo,* the butler's the murderer. It doesn't fit. No, it doesn't fit. You can't leave that other death out of account—the one down at my place."

"You're still of the opinion that the two are connected?"

Mr. Satterthwaite asked the question, though he had already answered it in the affirmative in his own mind.

"Man, they must be connected. Everything points to it. We've got to find the common factor—someone who was present on both occasions."

"Yes," said Mr. Satterthwaite. "And that's not going to be so simple a matter as one might think on the face of it. We've got too many common factors. Do you realize, Cartwright, that practically every person who was present at the dinner at your house was present here?"

Sir Charles nodded.

"Of course I've realized that, but do you realize what deduction one can draw from it?"

"I don't quite follow you, Cartwright."

"Dash it all, man; do you suppose that's coincidence? No, it was meant. Why are all the people who were at the

58

first death present at the second? Accident? Not on your life. It was plain—design—Tollie's plan."

"Oh!" said Mr. Satterthwaite. "Yes, it's possible."

"It's certain. You didn't know Tollie as well as I did, Satterthwaite. He was a man who kept his own counsel, and a very patient man. In all the years I've known him, I've never known Tollie to give utterance to a rash opinon or judgment.

"Look at it this way: Babbington's murdered—yes, murdered; I'm not going to hedge or mince terms—murdered one evening in my house. Tollie ridicules me gently for my suspicions in the matter, but all the time he's got suspicions of his own. He doesn't talk about them—that's not his way. But quietly, in his own mind, he's building up a case. I don't know what he had to build upon. It can't, I think, be a case against any one particular person. He believed that one of those people was responsible for the crime, and he made a plan, a test of some kind, to find out which person it was."

"What about the other guests—the Edens and the Cambells?"

"Camouflage. It made the whole thing less obvious."

"What do you think the plan was?"

Sir Charles shrugged his shoulders—an exaggerated foreign gesture. He was Aristide Duval, that master mind of the secret service. His left foot limped as he walked.

"How can we know? I am not a magician. I cannot guess. But there was a plan. It went wrong because the murderer was just one degree cleverer than Tollie thought. He struck first."

"He?"

"Or she. Poison is as much a woman's weapon as a man's—more so."

Mr. Satterthwaite was silent. Sir Charles said:

"Come now, don't you agree? Or are you on the side of public opinion? 'The butler's the man. He done it.' "

"What's your explanation of the butler?"

"I haven't thought about him. In my view, he doesn't matter. I could suggest an explanation."

"Such as?"

"Well, say that the police are right so far; Ellis is a

59

professional criminal, working in—shall we say?—with a gang of burglars. Ellis obtains this post with false credentials. Then Tollie is murdered. What is Ellis's position? A man is killed, and in the house is a man whose fingerprints are at Scotland Yard and who is known to the police. Naturally, he gets the wind up and bolts."

"But the secret passage."

"Secret passage be damned. He dodged out of the house while one of the fat-headed constables who were watching the house was taking forty winks."

"It certainly seems more probable."

"Well, Satterthwaite, what's your view?"

"Mine?" said Mr. Satterthwaite. "Oh, it's the same as yours. It has been all along. The butler seems to me a very clumsy red herring. I believe that Sir Bartholomew and poor old Babbington were killed by the same person."

"One of the house party?"

"One of the house party."

There was silence for a minute or two, and then Mr. Satterthwaite asked casually:

"Which of them do you think it was?"

"My God, Satterthwaite, how can I tell?"

"You can't tell, of course," said Mr. Satterthwaite mildly. "I just thought you might have some idea—you know, nothing scientific or reasoned. Just an ordinary guess."

"Well, I haven't." He thought for a minute, and then burst out: "You know, Satterthwaite, the moment you begin to think, it seems impossible that any of them did it."

"I suppose your theory is right," mused Mr. Satterthwaite. "As to the assembling of the suspects, I mean. We've got to take it into account that there were certain definite exclusions. Yourself and myself and Mrs. Babbington, for instance. Young Manders, too; he was out of it."

"Manders?"

"Yes, his arrival on the scene was an accident. He wasn't asked or expected. That lets him out of the circle of suspects."

"The dramatist woman too. Anthony Astor."

"No, no, she was there. Miss Muriel Wills, of Tooting."

"So she was. I'd forgotten the woman's name was Wills."

He frowned. Mr. Satterthwaite was fairly good at reading people's thoughts. He estimated with fair accuracy what was passing through the actor's mind. When the other spoke, Mr. Satterthwaite mentally patted himself on the back.

"You know, Satterthwaite, you're right. I don't think it was definitely suspected people that he asked, because, after all, Lady Mary and Egg were there. No, he wanted to stage some reproduction of the first business, perhaps. He suspected someone, but he wanted other eyewitnesses there to confirm matters. Something of that kind."

"Something of the kind," agreed Mr. Satterthwaite. "One can only generalize at this stage. Very well, the Lytton Gores are out of it; you and I and Mrs. Babbington and Oliver Manders are out of it. Who is left? Angela Sutcliffe?"

"Angie? My dear fellow. She's been a friend of Tollie's for years."

"Then it boils down to the Dacreses. In fact, Cartwright, you suspect the Dacreses. You might just as well have said so when I asked you."

Sir Charles looked at him. Mr. Satterthwaite had a mildly triumphant air.

"I suppose," said Cartwright slowly, "that I do. At least, I don't suspect them; they just seem rather more possible than anyone else. I don't know them very well, for one thing. But for the life of me, I can't see why Freddie Dacres, who spends his life on the race course, or Cynthia, who spends her time designing fabulously expensive clothes for women, should have any desire to remove a dear, insignificant old clergyman."

He shook his head, then his face brightened.

"There's the Wills woman. I forgot her again. What is there about her that continually makes you forget her? She's the most damnably nondescript creature I've ever seen."

Mr. Satterthwaite smiled.

"I rather fancy she might embody Burns's famous line, 'A chiel's amang ye takin' notes.' I rather fancy that Miss Wills spends her time taking notes. There are sharp eyes behind that pair of glasses. I think you'll find that anything worth noticing in this affair has been noticed by Miss Wills."

"Do you?" said Sir Charles doubtfully.

"The next thing to do," said Mr. Satterthwaite, "is to have some lunch. After that, we'll go out to the abbey and see what we can discover on the spot."

"You seem to be taking very kindly to this, Satterthwaite," said Sir Charles, with a twinkle of amusement.

"The investigation of crime is not new to me," said Mr. Satterthwaite. "Once when my car broke down and I was staying at a lonely inn——"

He got no further.

"I remember," said Sir Charles, in his high, clear, carrying actor's voice, "when I was touring in 1921——"

Sir Charles won.

CHAPTER IX

NOTHING could have been more peaceful than the grounds and building of Melfort Abbey as the two men saw it that afternoon in the September sunshine.

Portions of the abbey were fifteenth century. It had been restored and a new wing added on to it. The new sanatorium was out of sight of the house, with grounds of its own.

Sir Charles and Mr. Satterthwaite were received by Mrs. Leckie, the cook, a portly lady, decorously gowned in black, who was tearful and voluble. Sir Charles she already knew, and it was to him she addressed most of her conversation:

"You'll understand, I'm sure, sir, what it's meant to me. The master's death and all. Policemen all over the place, poking their noses here and there. Would you believe it, even the dustbins they had to have their noses in. And questions— they wouldn't have done with asking questions. Oh, that I should have lived to see such a thing—the doctor such a quiet gentleman as he always was, and made Sir Bartholomew, too, which a proud day it was to all of us, as Beatrice and I well remember, though she's been here two years less than I have. And such questions as that police fellow—for 'gentleman' I will not call him, having been accustomed to gentlemen and their ways, and knowing what's what—fellow, I say, whether or no he is a superintendent."

Mrs. Leckie paused, took breath and extricated herself from the somewhat complicated conversational morass into which she had fallen: "Questions, that's what I say, about all the maids in the house—and good girls they are, every one of them—not that I'd say that Doris gets up when she should do

63

in the morning. I have to speak about it at least once a week; and Vickie, she's inclined to be impertinent, but there, with the young ones you can't expect the training—their mothers don't give it to them nowadays—but good girls they are and no police superintendent shall make me say otherwise. 'Yes,' I said to him, 'you needn't think I'm going to say anything against my girls. They're good girls, they are, and as to having anything to do with murder, why, it's downright wicked to suggest such a thing.' "

Mrs. Leckie paused.

"Mr. Ellis, now, that's different. I don't know anything about Mr. Ellis and couldn't answer for him in any way, he having been brought from London and strange to the place, while Mr. Baker was on holiday."

"Baker?" asked Mr. Satterthwaite.

"Mr. Baker had been Sir Bartholomew's butler for the last seven years, sir. He was in London most of the time, in Harley Street. You'll remember him, sir?" She appealed to Sir Charles, who nodded. "Sir Bartholomew used to bring him up here when he had a party. But he hadn't been so well in his health, so Sir Bartholomew said, and he gave him a couple of months' holiday, paid for him, too, in a place near the sea down near Brighton—a real kind gentleman the doctor was—and he took Mr. Ellis on temporary for the time being, and so, as I said to that superintendent, I can't say anything about Mr. Ellis, though from all he said himself, he seems to have been with the best families, and he certainly had a gentlemanly way with him."

"You didn't find anything unusual about him?" asked Sir Charles hopefully.

"Well, it's odd your saying that, sir, because if you know what I mean, I did and I didn't."

Sir Charles looked encouraging and Mrs. Leckie went on:

"I couldn't exactly say what it was, sir, but there was something—"

"There always is—after the event," thought Mr. Satterthwaite to himself grimly. However much Mrs. Leckie had despised the police, she was not proof against suggestion. If Ellis turned out to be criminal, well, Mrs. Leckie would have noticed something.

"For one thing, he was standoffish. Oh, quite polite,

quite the gentleman—as I said, he'd been used to good houses. But he kept himself to himself, spent a lot of time in his own room. And he was—well, I don't know how to describe it, I'm sure—he was—well, there was something——"

"You didn't suspect he wasn't—not really a butler?" suggested Mr. Satterthwaite.

"Oh, he'd been in service right enough, sir. The things he knew—and about well-known people in society too."

"Such as?" suggested Sir Charles gently.

But Mrs. Leckie became vague and noncommittal. She was not going to retail servants' hall gossip. Such a thing would have offended her sense of fitness.

To put her at her ease, Mr. Satterthwaite said:

"Perhaps you can describe his appearance."

Mrs. Leckie brightened.

"Yes, indeed, sir. He was a very respectable-looking man— side whiskers and gray hair, stooped a little, and he was growing stout—it worried him, that did. He had rather a shaky hand, too, but not from the cause you might imagine. He was a most abstemious man—not like many I've known. His eyes were a bit weak, I think, sir; the light hurt them— especially a bright light used to make them water something cruel. Out with us he wore glasses, but not when he was on duty."

"No special distinguishing marks?" asked Sir Charles. "No scars? Or broken fingers? Or birthmarks?"

"Oh, no, sir; nothing of that kind."

"How superior detective stories are to life," sighed Sir Charles. "In fiction there is always some distinguishing characteristic."

"He had a tooth missing," said Mr. Satterthwaite.

"I believe so, sir. I never noticed it myself."

"What was his manner on the night of the tragedy?" asked Mr. Satterthwaite in a slightly bookish manner.

"Well, really, sir, I couldn't say. I was busy, you see, in my kitchen. I hadn't time for noticing things."

"No, no, quite so."

"When the news came out that the master was dead, we were all struck all of a heap. I cried and couldn't stop, and so did Beatrice. The young ones, of course, were excited like, though very upset. Mr. Ellis, naturally, wasn't so upset as we

65

were, he being new, but he behaved very considerate, and insisted on Beatrice and me taking a little glass of port to counteract the shock. And to think that all the time it was he—the villain——"

Words failed Mrs. Leckie, her eyes shone with indignation.

"He disappeared that night, I understand?"

"Yes, sir, went to his room like the rest of us, and in the morning he wasn't there. That's what set the police on him, of course."

"Yes, yes, very foolish of him. Have you any idea how he left the house?"

"Not the slightest. It seems the police were watching the house all night, and they never saw him go—but there, that's what the police are, human like anyone else, in spite of the airs that they give themselves, coming into a gentleman's house and nosing round."

"I hear there's some question of a secret passage," Sir Charles said.

Mrs. Leckie sniffed.

"That's what the police say."

"Is there such a thing?"

"I've heard mention of it," Mrs. Leckie agreed cautiously.

"Do you know where it starts from?"

"No, I don't, sir. Secret passages are all very well, but they're not things to be encouraged in the servants' hall. It gives the girls ideas. They might think of slipping out that way. My girls go out by the back door and in by the back door, and then we know where we are."

"Splendid, Mrs. Leckie. I think you're very wise."

Mrs. Leckie bridled in the sun of Sir Charles's approval.

"I wonder," he went on, "if we might just ask a few questions of the other servants?"

"Of course, sir, but they can't tell you anything more than I can."

"Oh, I know. I didn't mean so much about Ellis as about Sir Bartholomew himself—his manner that night, and so on. You see, he was a friend of mine."

"I know, sir. I quite understand. There's Beatrice, and there's Doris. She waited at table, of course."

"Yes, I'd like to see Doris."

66

Mrs. Leckie, however, had a belief in seniority. Beatrice Church, the upper housemaid, was the first to appear.

She was a tall, thin woman with a pinched mouth, who looked aggressively respectable.

After a few unimportant questions, Sir Charles led the talk to the behavior of the house party on the fatal evening. Had they all been terribly upset? What had they said or done?

A little animation entered into Beatrice's manner. She had the usual ghoulish relish for tragedy.

"Miss Sutcliffe, she quite broke down. A very warm-hearted lady, she's stayed here before. I suggested bringing her a little drop of brandy, or a nice cup of tea, but she wouldn't hear of it. She took some aspirin, though. Said she was sure she couldn't sleep. But she was sleeping like a little child the next morning when I brought her her early tea."

"And Mrs. Dacres?"

"I don't think anything would upset that lady much."

From Beatrice's tone, she had not liked Cynthia Dacres.

"Just anxious to get away, she was. Said her business would suffer. She's a big dressmaker in London, so Mr. Ellis told us."

A big dressmaker, to Beatrice, meant "trade," and "trade" she looked down upon.

"And her husband?"

Beatrice sniffed.

"Steadied his nerves with brandy, he did. Or unsteadied them, some would say."

"What about Lady Mary Lytton Gore?"

"A very nice lady," said Beatrice, her tone softening. "My great-aunt was in service with her father at the castle. A pretty young girl she was, so I've always heard. Poor she may be, but you can see she's someone—and so considerate, never giving trouble and always speaking so pleasant. Her daughter's a nice young lady too. They didn't know Sir Bartholomew well, of course, but they were very distressed."

"Miss Wills?"

Some of Beatrice's rigidity returned.

"I'm sure I couldn't say, sir, what Miss Wills thought about it."

"Or what you thought about her?" asked Sir Charles. "Come now, Beatrice, be human."

An unexpected smile dinted Beatrice's wooden cheeks. There was something appealingly schoolboyish in Sir Charles's manner. She was not proof against the charm that nightly audiences had felt so strongly.

"Really, sir, I don't know what you want me to say."

"Just what you thought and felt about Miss Wills."

"Nothing, sir—nothing at all. She wasn't, of course——" Beatrice hesitated.

"Go on, Beatrice."

"Well, she wasn't quite the class of the others, sir. She couldn't help it, I know," went on Beatrice kindly. "But she did things a real lady wouldn't have done. She pried, if you know what I mean, sir—poked and pried about."

Sir Charles tried hard to get this statement amplified, but Beatrice remained vague. Miss Wills had poked and pried; but asked to produce a special instance of the poking, Beatrice seemed unable to do so. She merely repeated that Miss Wills pried into things that were no business of hers.

They gave it up at last and Mr. Satterthwaite said:

"Young Mr. Manders arrived unexpectedly, didn't he?"

"Yes, sir, he had an accident with his motorcycle—just by the lodge gates, it was. He said it was a bit of luck, its happening just here. The house was full, of course, but Miss Lyndon had a bed made up for him in the little study."

"Was everyone very surprised to see him?"

"Oh, yes, sir; naturally, sir."

Asked her opinion of Ellis, Beatrice was noncommittal. She'd seen very little of him. Going off the way he did looked bad; though why he should want to harm the master, she couldn't imagine. Nobody could.

"What was he like—the doctor, I mean? Did he seem to be looking forward to the house party? Had he anything on his mind?"

"He seemed particularly cheerful, sir. Smiled to himself, he did, as though he had some joke on. I even heard him make a joke with Mr. Ellis—a thing he'd never done with Mr. Baker. He was usually a bit brusque with the servants, kind always, but not speaking to them much."

"What did he say?" asked Mr. Satterthwaite eagerly.

"Well, I forget exactly now, sir. Mr. Ellis had come up with a telephone message, and Sir Bartholomew asked him if he was sure he'd got the names right, and Mr. Ellis said quite sure—speaking respectful, of course. And the doctor, he laughed and said, 'You're a good fellow, Ellis, a first-class butler. . . . Eh, Beatrice, what do you think?' And I was so surprised, sir, at the master speaking like that—quite unlike his usual self—that I didn't know what to say."

"And Ellis?"

"He looked kind of disapproving, sir. As though it was the kind of thing he hadn't been used to. Stiff like."

"What was the telephone message?" asked Sir Charles.

"The message, sir? Oh, it was from the sanatorium—about a patient who had arrived there and had stood the journey well."

"Do you remember the name?"

"It was a queer name, sir," Beatrice hesitated. "Mrs. de Rushbridger—something like that."

"Ah, yes," said Sir Charles soothingly. "Not an easy name to get right on the telephone. Well, thank you very much, Beatrice. Perhaps we could see Doris now."

When Beatrice had left the room, Sir Charles and Mr. Satterthwaite compared notes by an interchange of glances.

"Miss Wills poked and pried, Captain Dacres got drunk, Mrs. Dacres displayed no emotion. Anything there? Precious little."

"Very little indeed," agreed Mr. Satterthwaite.

"Let's pin our hopes on Doris."

Doris was a demure, dark-eyed young woman of thirty. She was only too pleased to talk.

She herself didn't believe Mr. Ellis had anything to do with it. He was too much the gentleman. The police had suggested he was just a common crook. Doris was sure he was nothing of the sort.

"You're quite certain he was an ordinary honest-to-God butler?" asked Sir Charles.

"Not ordinary, sir. He wasn't like any butler that I've ever worked with before. He arranged the work different."

"But you don't think he poisoned your master."

"Oh, sir, I don't see how he could have done. I was

69

waiting at table with him, and he couldn't have put anything in the master's food without my seeing him."

"And the drink?"

"He went round with the wine, sir. Sherry first, with the soup, and then hock and claret. But what could he have done, sir? If there'd been anything in the wine, he'd have poisoned everybody—or all those who took it. It's not as though the master had anything that nobody else had. The same thing with the port. All the gentlemen had port, and some of the ladies."

"The wineglasses were taken out on a tray?"

"Yes, sir, I held the tray and Mr. Ellis put the glasses on it, and I carried the tray out to the pantry, and there they were, sir, when the police came to examine them. The port glasses were still on the table. And the police didn't find anything."

"You're quite sure that the doctor didn't have anything to eat or drink at dinner that nobody else had?"

"Not that I saw, sir. In fact, I'm sure he didn't."

"Nothing that one of the guests gave him?"

"Oh, no, sir."

"Do you know anything about a secret passage, Doris?"

"One of the gardeners told me something about it. Comes out in the wood where there's some old walls and things tumbled down. But I've never seen any opening to it in the house."

"Ellis never said anything about it?"

"Oh, no, sir; he wouldn't know anything about it, I'm sure."

"Who do you really think killed your master, Doris?"

"I don't know, sir. I can't believe anyone did. I feel it must have been some kind of accident."

"H'm, thank you, Doris."

"If it wasn't for the death of Babbington," said Sir Charles, as the girl left the room, "we could make her the criminal. She's a good-looking girl. And she waited at table. . . . No, it won't do. Babbington was murdered. And anyway, Tollie never noticed good-looking girls. He wasn't made that way."

"But he was fifty-five," said Mr. Satterthwaite thoughtfully.

"Why do you say that?"

"It's the age when a man loses his head badly about a girl, even if he hasn't done so before."

"Dash it all, Satterthwaite, I'm—er—getting on for fifty-five."

"I know," said Mr. Satterthwaite.

And before his gentle twinkling gaze, Sir Charles's eyes fell.

He looked consciously confused.

CHAPTER X

"How about an examination of Ellis's room?" asked Mr. Satterthwaite, having enjoyed the spectacle of Sir Charles's blush to the full.

The actor seized at the diversion:

"Excellent, excellent. Just what I was about to suggest myself."

"Of course the police have already searched it thoroughly."

"The police—"

Aristide Duval waved the police away scornfully. Anxious to forget his momentary discomfiture, he flung himself with renewed vigor into his part.

"The police are blockheads," he said sweepingly. "What have they looked for in Ellis's room? Evidences of his guilt. We shall look for evidences of his innocence. An entirely different thing."

"You're completely convinced of Ellis's innocence?"

"If we're right about Babbington, he must be innocent."

"Yes, besides——"

Mr. Satterthwaite did not finish his sentence. He had been about to say that if Ellis was a professional criminal who had been detected by Sir Bartholomew and had murdered him in consequence, the whole affair would become unbearably dull. Just in time he remembered that Sir Bartholomew had been a friend of Charles Cartwright's, and was duly appalled by the callousness of the sentiments he had nearly revealed.

At first sight, Ellis's room did not seem to offer much promise of discovery. The clothes in the drawers and hanging

72

in the cupboard were all neatly arranged. They were well cut and bore different tailors' marks. Clearly, cast-offs given him in different situations. The underclothing was on the same scale. The boots were neatly polished and arranged on trees.

Mr. Satterthwaite picked up a boot and murmured: "Nines—just so, nines." But, since there were no footprints in the case, that didn't seem to lead anywhere.

It seemed clear, from its absence, that Ellis had departed in his butler's kit, and Mr. Satterthwaite pointed out to Sir Charles that that seemed rather a remarkable fact.

"Any man in his senses would have changed into an ordinary suit."

"Yes, it's odd, that. Looks almost—though that's absurd—as if he hadn't gone at all. Nonsense, of course."

They continued their search. No letters, no papers, except a cutting from a newspaper regarding a cure for corns, and a paragraph relating to the approaching marriage of a duke's daughter.

There was a small blotting book and a penny bottle of ink on a side table; no pen. Sir Charles held up the blotting book to the mirror, but without result. One page of it was very much used—a meaningless jumble—and the ink looked, to both men, old.

"Either he hasn't written any letters since he was here or he hadn't blotted them," deduced Mr. Satterthwaite. "This is an old blotter. Ah, yes." With some gratification, he pointed to a barely decipherable "L. Baker" amidst the jumble.

"I should say that Ellis hadn't used this at all."

"That's rather odd, isn't it?" said Sir Charles.

"What do you mean?"

"Well, a man usually writes letters."

"Not if he's a criminal."

"No, perhaps you're right. There must have been something fishy about him to make him bolt as he did. All we say is that he didn't murder Tollie."

They hunted round the floor, raising the carpet, looking under the bed. There was nothing anywhere except a splash of ink beside the fireplace. The room was disappointingly bare.

They left it in a somewhat disconcerted fashion. Their zeal as detectives was momentarily damped.

Possibly the thought passed through their minds that things were arranged better in books.

They had a few words with the other members of the staff, scared-looking juniors in awe of Mrs. Leckie and Beatrice Church, but they elicited nothing further.

Finally they took their leave.

"Well, Satterthwaite," said Sir Charles, as they strolled across the park—Mr. Satterthwaite's car had been instructed to pick them up at the lodge—"anything strike you—anything at all?"

Mr. Satterthwaite thought. He was not to be hurried into an answer—especially as he felt something ought to have struck him. To confess that the whole expedition had been a waste of time was an unwelcome idea. He passed over in his mind the evidence of one servant after another; the information was extraordinarily meager.

As Sir Charles had summed it up just now, Miss Wills had poked and pried, Miss Sutcliffe had been very upset. Mrs. Dacres had not been upset at all, and Captain Dacres had got drunk. Very little there, unless Freddie Dacres's indulgence showed the deadening of a guilty conscience. But Freddie Dacres, Mr. Satterthwaite knew, quite frequently got drunk.

"Well?" repeated Sir Charles impatiently.

"Nothing," confessed Mr. Satterthwaite reluctantly, "except—well, I think we are entitled to assume, from the clipping we found, that Ellis suffered from corns."

Sir Charles gave a wry smile.

"That seems quite a reasonable deduction. Does it—er—get us anywhere?"

Mr. Satterthwaite confessed that it did not.

"The only other thing," he said, and then stopped.

"Yes? Go on, man. Anything may help."

"It struck me as a little odd the way that Sir Bartholomew chaffed his butler—you know, what the household told us. It seems, somehow, uncharacteristic."

"It was uncharacteristic," said Sir Charles with emphasis. "I knew Tollie well—better than you did—and I can tell you that he wasn't a facetious sort of man. He'd never have spoken like that unless—well, unless, for some reason, he wasn't quite normal at the time. You're right, Satterthwaite; that is a point. Now where does it get us?"

"Well——" began Mr. Satterthwaite, but it was clear that Sir Charles's question had been merely a rhetorical one. He was anxious, not to hear Mr. Satterthwaite's views, but to air his own.

"You remember when that incident occurred, Satterthwaite? Just after Ellis had brought him a telephone message. I think it's a fair deduction to assume that it was that telephone message which was the cause of Tollie's sudden unusual hilarity. You may remember I asked the housemaid woman what that message had been."

Mr. Satterthwaite nodded.

"It was to say that a woman named Mrs. de Rushbridger had arrived at the sanatorium," he said, to show that he, too, had paid attention to the point. "It doesn't sound particularly thrilling."

"It doesn't sound so, certainly. But if our reasoning is correct, there must be some significance in that message."

"Ye-es," said Mr. Satterthwaite doubtfully.

"Indubitably," said Sir Charles. "We've got to find out what that significance was. It just crosses my mind that it may have been a code message of some kind—a harmless-sounding, natural thing, but which really meant something entirely different. If Tollie had been making inquiries into Babbington's death, this may have had something to do with those inquiries. Say, even, that he employed a private detective to find out a certain fact. He may have told him, in the event of this particular suspicion being justified, to ring up and use that particular phrase, which would convey no hint of the truth to anyone taking it. That would explain his jubilation; it might explain his asking Ellis if he was sure of the name; he himself knowing well there was no such person really. In fact, the slight lack of balance a person shows when he has brought off what can be described as a long shot."

"You think there's no such person as Mrs. de Rushbridger?"

"Well, I think we ought to find out for certain."

"How?"

"We might run along to the sanatorium now and ask the matron."

"She may think it rather odd."

Sir Charles laughed.

"You leave it to me," he said.

They turned aside from the drive and walked in the direction of the sanatorium.

Mr. Satterthwaite said:

"What about you, Cartwright? Does anything strike you at all? Arising out of our visit to the house, I mean?"

Sir Charles answered slowly: "Yes, there is something. The devil of it is, I can't remember what."

Mr. Satterthwaite stared at him in surprise. The other frowned.

"How can I explain? There was something—something which, at the moment, struck me as wrong, as unlikely—only, I hadn't the time to think about it then. I put it aside in my own mind."

"And now you can't remember what it was?"

"No. Only that at some moment I said to myself, 'That's odd.' "

"Was it when we were questioning the servants? Which servant?"

"I tell you I can't remember. And the more I think the less I shall remember. If I leave it alone, it may come back to me."

They came into view of the sanatorium, a big white modern building, divided from the park by palings. There was a gate through which they passed, and they rang the front doorbell and asked for the matron.

The matron, when she came, was a tall, middle-aged woman, with an intelligent face and a capable manner. Sir Charles she clearly knew by name as a friend of the late Sir Bartholomew Strange.

Sir Charles explained that he had just come back from abroad, had been horrified to hear of his friend's death and of the terrible suspicions entertained, and had been up to the house to learn as many details as he could. The matron spoke in moving terms of the loss Sir Bartholomew would be to them, and of his fine career as a doctor. Sir Charles professed himself anxious to know what was going to happen to the sanatorium. The matron explained that Sir Bartholomew had

had two partners, both capable doctors; one was in residence at the sanatorium.

"Bartholomew was very proud of this place, I know," said Sir Charles.

"Yes, his treatments were a great success."

"Mostly nerve cases, isn't it?"

"Yes."

"That reminds me; fellow I met out at Monte had some kind of relation coming here. I forget her name now—odd sort of name—Rushbridger—Rushbridger—something like that."

"Mrs. de Rushbridger, you mean?"

"That's it. Is she here now?"

"Oh, yes. But I'm afraid she won't be able to see you—not for some time yet. She's having a very strict rest cure." The matron smiled just a trifle archly. "No letters, no exciting visitors."

"I say, she's not very bad, is she?"

"Rather a bad nervous breakdown—lapses of memory and severe nervous exhaustion. Oh, we shall get her right in time."

The matron smiled reassuringly.

"Let me see. Haven't I heard Tollie—Sir Bartholomew—speak of her? She was a friend of his as well as a patient, wasn't she?"

"I don't think so, Sir Charles. At least the doctor never said so. She has recently arrived from the West Indies. Really, it was very funny, I must tell you. Rather a difficult name for a servant to remember—the parlormaid here is rather stupid. She came and said to me: 'Mrs. West India has come,' and of course I suppose Rushbridger does sound rather like West India; but it was rather a coincidence, her having just come from the West Indies."

"Rather, rather; most amusing. Her husband over too?"

"He's still out there."

"Ah, quite, quite. I must be mixing her up with someone else. It was a case the doctor was specially interested in."

"Cases of amnesia are fairly common, but they're always interesting to a medical man—the variations, you know. Two cases are seldom alike."

"Seems all very odd to me. . . . Well, thank you, matron. I'm glad to have had a little chat with you. I know how much

77

Tollie thought of you. He often spoke about you," finished Sir Charles mendaciously.

"Oh, I'm glad to hear that." The matron flushed and bridled. "Such a splendid man; such a loss to us all. We were absolutely shocked—well, stunned would describe it better. Murder! 'Whoever would murder Doctor Strange?' I said. It's incredible. That awful butler. I hope the police catch him. And no motive or anything."

Sir Charles shook his head sadly and they took their departure, going round by the road to the spot where the car awaited them.

In revenge for his enforced quiescence during the interview with the matron, Mr. Satterthwaite displayed a lively interest in the scene of Oliver Manders's accident, plying the lodge keeper, a slow-witted man of middle age, with questions.

Yes, that was the place, where the wall was broken away. On a motorcycle the young gentleman was. No, he didn't see it happen. He heard it, though, and come out to see. The young gentleman was standing there—just where the other gentleman was standing now. He didn't seem to be hurt. Just looking rueful like at his bike—and a proper mess that was. Just asked what the name of the place might be, and when he heard it was Sir Bartholomew Strange's, he said, "That's a piece of luck," and went on up to the house. A very calm young gentleman he seemed to be—tired like. How he come to have such an accident the lodge keeper couldn't see, but he supposed them things went wrong sometimes.

"It was an odd accident," said Mr. Satterthwaite thoughtfully.

He looked at the wide straight road. No bends, no dangerous crossroads, nothing to cause a motorcyclist to swerve suddenly into a ten-foot wall. Yes, an odd accident.

"What's in your mind, Satterthwaite?" asked Sir Charles curiously.

"Nothing," said Mr. Satterthwaite. "Nothing."

"It's odd, certainly," said Sir Charles, and he, too, stared at the scene of the accident in a puzzled manner.

They got into the car and drove off.

Mr. Satterthwaite was busy with his thoughts. Mrs. de Rushbridger. . . . Cartwright's theory wouldn't work; it wasn't a code message. There was such a person. But could there be something about the woman herself? Was she, perhaps, a witness of some kind? Or was it just because she was an interesting case that Bartholomew Strange had displayed this unusual elation? Was she, perhaps, an attractive woman? To fall in love at the age of fifty-five did—Mr. Satterthwaite had observed it many a time—change a man's character completely. It might, perhaps, make him facetious where, before, he had been aloof.

His thoughts were interrupted. Sir Charles leaned forward.

"Satterthwaite," he said, "do you mind if we turn back?"

Without waiting for a reply, he took up the speaking tube and gave the order. The car slowed down, stopped, and the chauffeur began to reverse into a convenient lane. A minute or two later they were bowling along the road in the opposite direction.

"What is it?" asked Mr. Satterthwaite.

"I've just remembered," said Sir Charles, "what it was that struck me as odd. It was the ink stain on the floor in the butler's room."

CHAPTER XI

M R. Satterthwaite stared at his friend in surprise.

"The ink stain? What do you mean, Cartwright?"

"You remember it?"

"I remember there was an ink stain, yes."

"You remember its position?"

"Well, not exactly."

"It was close to the skirting board near the fireplace."

"Yes, so it was. I remember now."

"How do you think that stain was caused, Satterthwaite?"

Mr. Satterthwaite reflected a minute or two.

"It wasn't a big stain," he said at last. "It couldn't have been an upset ink bottle. I should say, in all probability, that the man dropped his fountain pen there. There was no pen in the room, you remember." ["He shall see that I notice things just as much as he does," thought Mr. Satterthwaite.] "So it seems clear that the man must have had a fountain pen if he ever wrote at all, and there's no evidence that he ever did."

"Yes, there is, Satterthwaite. There's the ink stain."

"He mayn't have been writing," snapped Mr. Satterthwaite. "He may have just dropped the pen on the floor."

"But there wouldn't have been a stain unless the top had been off the pen."

"I dare say you're right," said Mr. Satterthwaite. "But I can't see what's odd about it."

"Perhaps there isn't anything odd," said Sir Charles. "I can't tell till I get back and see for myself."

They were turning in at the lodge gates. A few minutes later they had arrived at the house, and Sir Charles was allaying the curiosity caused by his return by inventing a pencil left behind in the butler's room.

"And now," said Sir Charles, shutting the door of Ellis's room behind them, having, with some skill, shaken off the helpful Mrs. Leckie, "let's see if I'm making an infernal fool of myself, or whether there's anything in my idea."

In Mr. Satterthwaite's opinion, the former alternative was by far the more probable, but he was much too polite to say so. He sat down on the bed and watched the other.

"Here's our stain," said Sir Charles, indicating the mark with his foot. "Right up against the skirting board at the opposite side of the room to the writing table. Under what circumstances would a man drop a pen just there?"

"You can drop a pen anywhere," said Mr. Satterthwaite.

"You can hurl it across the room, of course," agreed Sir Charles. "But one doesn't usually treat one's pen like that. I don't know, though. Fountain pens are damned annoying things. Dry up and refuse to write just when you most want them to. Perhaps that's the solution of the matter. Ellis lost his temper, said, 'Damn the thing,' and hurled it across the room."

"I think there are plenty of explanations," said Mr. Satterthwaite. "He may have simply laid the pen on the mantelpiece and it rolled off."

Sir Charles experimented with a pencil. He allowed it to roll off the corner of the mantelpiece. The pencil struck the ground at least a foot from the mark and rolled inwards toward the gas fire.

"Well," said Mr. Satterthwaite, "what's your explanation?"

"I'm trying to find one."

From his seat on the bed, Mr. Satterthwaite now witnessed a thoroughly amusing performance.

Sir Charles tried dropping the pencil from his hand as he walked in the direction of the fireplace. He tried sitting on the edge of the bed and writing there, and then dropping the pencil. To get the pencil to fall on the right spot, it was necessary to stand or sit jammed up against the wall in a most unconvincing attitude.

"That's impossible," said Sir Charles aloud. He stood considering the wall, the stain and the prim little gas fire.

"If he were burning papers, now," he said thoughtfully. "But one doesn't burn papers in a gas fire."

Suddenly Sir Charles drew in his breath.

A minute later Mr. Satterthwaite was realizing Sir Charles's profession to the full.

Charles Cartwright had become Ellis, the butler. He sat writing at the writing table. He looked furtive; every now and then he raised his eyes, shooting them shiftily from side to side. Suddenly he seemed to hear something. Mr. Satterthwaite could even guess what that something was—footsteps along the passage. The man had a guilty conscience. He attached a certain meaning to those footsteps. He sprang up, the paper on which he had been writing in one hand, his pen in the other. He darted across the room to the fireplace, his head half turned, still alert, listening, afraid. He tried to shove the papers under the gas fire; in order to use both hands, he cast down the pen impatiently. Sir Charles's pencil, the pen of the drama, fell accurately on the ink stain.

"Bravo!" said Mr. Satterthwaite, applauding generously.

So good had the performance been that he was left with the impression that so, and only so, could Ellis have acted.

"You see?" said Sir Charles, resuming his own personality and speaking with modest elation. "If the fellow heard the police, or what he thought was the police, coming and had to hide what he was writing—well, where could he hide it? Not in a drawer or under the mattress. If the police searched the room, that would be found at once. He hadn't time to take up a floor board. No, behind the gas fire was the only chance."

"The next thing to do," said Mr. Satterthwaite, "is to see whether there is anything hidden behind the gas fire."

"Exactly. Of course, it may have been a false alarm and he may have got the things out again later. But we'll hope for the best."

Removing his coat and turning up his shirt sleeves, Sir Charles lay down on the floor and applied his eye to the crack under the gas fire.

"There's something under there," he reported. "Something white. How can we get it out? We want something like a woman's hatpin."

"Women don't have hatpins anymore," said Mr. Satterthwaite sadly. "Perhaps a penknife."

But a penknife proved unavailing.

In the end, Mr. Satterthwaite went out and borrowed a

knitting needle from Beatrice. Though extremely curious to know what he wanted it for, her sense of decorum was too great to permit her to ask.

The knitting needle did the trick. Sir Charles extracted half a dozen sheets of crumpled writing paper, hastily crushed together and pushed in.

With growing excitement, he and Mr. Satterthwaite smoothed them out. They were clearly several different drafts of a letter, written in a small, neat, clerkly handwriting. The first began:

> This is to say that the writer of this does not wish to cause unpleasantness and may possibly have been mistaken in what he thought he saw tonight, but——

Here the writer had clearly been dissatisfied and had broken off to start afresh:

> John Ellis, butler, presents his compliments and would be glad of a short interview touching the tragedy tonight, before going to the police with certain information in his possession——

Still dissatisfied, the man had tried again:

> John Ellis, butler, has certain facts concerning the death of the doctor in his possession. He has not yet given these facts to the police——

In the next one the use of the third person had been abandoned:

> I am badly in need of money. A thousand pounds would make all the difference to me. There are certain things I could tell the police, but do not want to make trouble——

The last one was even more unreserved:

> I know how the doctor died. I haven't said anything to the police—yet. If you will meet me——

This letter broke off in a different way; after the "me," the pen had tailed off in a scrawl and the last five words were all blurred and blotchy. Clearly, it was when writing this that Ellis had heard something that alarmed him. He had crumpled up the papers and dashed to conceal them.

Mr. Satterthwaite drew a deep breath.

"I congratulate you, Cartwright," he said. "Your instinct about that ink stain was right. Good work. Now let's see exactly where we stand."

He paused a minute.

"Ellis, as we thought, is a scoundrel. He wasn't the murderer, but he knew who the murderer was, and he was preparing to blackmail him or her."

"Him or her," interrupted Sir Charles. "Annoying we don't know which. Why couldn't the fellow begin one of his effusions 'sir' or 'madam'; then we'd know where we are. Ellis seems to have been an artistic sort of fellow. He was taking a lot of trouble over his blackmailing letter. If only he'd given us one clue—one simple little clue—as to whom that letter was addressed to."

"Never mind," said Mr. Satterthwaite. "We are getting on. You remember you said that what we wanted to find in this room was a proof of Ellis's innocence. Well, we've found it. These letters show that he was innocent—of the murder, I mean. He was a thorough-paced scoundrel in other ways, but he didn't murder Sir Bartholomew Strange. Somebody else did that. Someone who murdered Babbington also. I think even the police will have to come round to our view now."

"You're going to tell them about this?" Sir Charles's voice expressed dissatisfaction.

"I don't see that we can do otherwise. Why?"

"Well——" Sir Charles sat down on the bed. His brow furrowed itself in thought. "How can I put it best? At the moment we know something that nobody else does. The police are looking for Ellis. They think he's the murderer. Everyone knows that they think he's the murderer. So the real criminal must be feeling pretty good. He or she will be not exactly off his or her guard, but feeling—well, comfortable. Isn't it a pity to upset that state of things? Isn't that just our chance? I mean our chance of finding a connection between Babbington and one of these people. They don't know that anyone has connected this death with Babbington's death. They'll be unsuspicious. It's a chance in a hundred."

"I see what you mean," said Mr. Satterthwaite. "And I agree with you. It is a chance. But all the same, I don't think we can take it. It is our duty as citizens to report this discovery of ours to the police at once. We have no right to withhold it from them."

Sir Charles looked at him quizzically.

"You're the pattern of a good citizen, Satterthwaite. I've no doubt the orthodox thing must be done, but I'm not nearly such a good citizen as you are. I should have no scruples in keeping this find to myself for a day or two—only a day or two, eh? . . . No? Well, I give in. Let us be pillars of law and order."

"You see," explained Mr. Satterthwaite, "Johnson is a friend of mine and he was very decent about it all—let us into all the police were doing: gave us full information and all that."

"Oh, you're right," sighed Sir Charles. "Quite right. Only, after all, no one but me thought of looking under that gas stove. The idea never occurred to one of those thick-headed policemen. But have it your own way. I say, Satterthwaite, where do you think Ellis is now?"

"I presume," said Mr. Satterthwaite, "that he got what he wanted. He was paid to disappear, and he did disappear, most effectually."

"Yes," said Sir Charles, "I suppose that is the explanation."

He gave a slight shiver.

"I don't like this room, Satterthwaite. Come out of it."

CHAPTER XII

SIR Charles and Mr. Satterthwaite arrived back in London the following evening.

The interview with Colonel Johnson had had to be very tactfully conducted. Superintendent Crossfield had not been too pleased that mere "gentlemen" should have found what he and his assistants had missed. He was at some pains to save his face.

"Very creditable indeed, sir. I confess I never thought of looking under the gas fire. As a matter of fact, it beats me what set you looking there."

The two men had not gone into a detailed account of how theorizing from an ink blot had led to the discovery. "Just nosing around" was how Sir Charles had put it.

"Still, look you did," continued the superintendent. "And were justified. Not that what you've found is much surprise to me. You see, it stands to reason that if Ellis wasn't the murderer, he must have disappeared for some reason or other, and it's been in the back of my mind all along that blackmail might have been his line of business."

One thing did arise from their discovery. Colonel Johnson was going to communicate with the Loomouth police. The death of Stephen Babbington ought certainly to be investigated.

"And if they find he died from nicotine poisoning, too, even Crossfield will admit the two deaths are connected," said Sir Charles, when they were speeding toward London.

He was still a little disgruntled at having had to hand over his discovery to the police.

Mr. Satterthwaite had soothed him by pointing out that

86

the information was not to be made public or given to the press.

"The guilty person will have no misgivings. The search for Ellis will still be continued."

Sir Charles admitted that that was true.

On arrival in London, he explained to Mr. Satterthwaite, he proposed to get in touch with Egg Lytton Gore. Her letter had been written from an address in Belgrave Square. He hoped that she might still be there.

Mr. Satterthwaite gravely approved this course. He himself was anxious to see Egg. It was arranged that Sir Charles should ring her up as soon as they reached London.

Egg proved to be still in town. She and her mother were staying with relatives and were not returning to Loomouth for about a week. Egg was easily prevailed upon to come out and dine with the two men.

"She can't come here very well, I suppose," said Sir Charles, looking round his luxurious flat. "Her mother mightn't like it, eh? Of course, we could have Miss Milray, too, but I'd rather not. To tell the truth, Miss Milray cramps my style a bit. She's so efficient that she gives me an inferiority complex."

Mr. Satterthwaite suggested his house. In the end it was arranged to dine at the Berkeley. Afterward, if Egg liked, they could adjourn elsewhere.

Mr. Satterthwaite noticed at once that the girl was looking thinner. Her eyes seemed larger and more feverish, her chin more decided. She was pale and had circles under her eyes. But her charm was as great as ever, her childish eagerness just as intense.

She said to Sir Charles, "I knew you'd come."

Her tone implied, "Now that you've come, everything will be all right."

Mr. Satterthwaite thought to himself: "But she wasn't sure he'd come; she wasn't sure at all. She's been on tenterhooks. She's been fretting herself to death." And he thought: "Doesn't the man realize? Actors are usually vain enough. Doesn't he know the girl's head over heels in love with him?"

It was, he thought, an odd situation. That Sir Charles was overwhelmingly in love with the girl was perfectly plain. She was equally in love with him. And the link between them—the link to which each of them clung frenziedly—was a crime—a double crime of a revolting nature.

During dinner little was said; Sir Charles talked about his experiences abroad. Egg talked about Loomouth. Mr. Satterthwaite encouraged them both whenever the conversation seemed likely to flag.

When dinner was over, they went to Mr. Satterthwaite's house.

Mr. Satterthwaite's house was on Chelsea Embankment. It was a large house and contained many beautiful works of art. There were pictures, sculpture, Chinese porcelain, prehistoric pottery, ivories, miniatures and much genuine Chippendale and Hepplewhite furniture. It had an atmosphere about it of mellowness and understanding.

Egg Lytton Gore saw nothing, noticed nothing. She flung off her evening coat onto a chair and said:

"At last. Now tell me all about it."

She listened with vivid interest whilst Sir Charles narrated their adventures in Yorkshire, drawing in her breath sharply when he described the discovery of the blackmailing letters.

"What happened after that we can only conjecture," finished Sir Charles. "Presumably, Ellis was paid to hold his tongue, and his escape was facilitated."

But Egg shook her head.

"Oh, no," she said. "Don't you see? Ellis is dead."

Both men were startled, but Egg reiterated her assertion:

"Of course he's dead. That's why he's disappeared so successfully that no one can find a trace of him. He knew too much, and so he was killed. Ellis is the third murder."

Although neither of the two men had considered the possibility before, they were forced to admit that it did not entirely ring false.

"But look here, my dear girl," argued Sir Charles. "It's all very well to say Ellis is dead. Where's the body? There's twelve stone or so of solid butler to be accounted for."

"I don't know where the body is," said Egg. "There must be lots of places."

"Hardly," murmured Mr. Satterthwaite. "Hardly."

"Lots," reitereated Egg. "Let me see." She paused for a moment. "Attics—there are masses of attics that no one ever goes into. He's probably in a trunk in the attic."

"Rather unlikely," said Sir Charles. "But possible, of course. It might evade discovery for—er—a time."

It was not Egg's way to avoid unpleasantness. She dealt immediately with the point in Sir Charles's mind:

"Smell goes up, not down. You'd notice a decaying body in the cellar much sooner than in the attic. And anyway, for a long time people would think it was a dead rat."

"If your theory were correct, it would point definitely to a man as the murderer. A woman couldn't drag a body round the house. In fact, it would be a pretty good feat for a man."

"Well, there are other possibilities. There's a secret passage there, you know. Miss Sutcliffe told me so. And Sir Bartholomew told me he would show it to me. The murderer might have given Ellis the money and shown him the way to get out of the house—gone down the passage with him—and killed him there. A woman could do that. She could stab him, or something, from behind. Then she'd just leave the body there and go back, and no one would ever know."

Sir Charles shook his head doubtfully, but he no longer disputed Egg's theory.

Mr. Satterthwaite felt sure that the same suspicion had come to him for a moment in Ellis's room when they had found the letters. He remembered Sir Charles' little shiver. The idea that Ellis might be dead had come to him then.

Mr. Satterthwaite thought: "If Ellis is dead, then we're dealing with a very dangerous person. Yes, a very dangerous person." And suddenly he felt a cold chill of fear down his spine.

A person who had killed three times wouldn't hesitate to kill again.

They were in danger, all three of them—Sir Charles, and Egg, and he.

If they found out too much——

He was recalled by the sound of Sir Charles's voice:

"There's one thing I didn't understand in your letter, Egg. You spoke of someone being in danger—of the police suspecting him. I can't see that they attach the least suspicion to anyone."

It seemed to Mr. Satterthwaite that Egg was very slightly discomposed. He even fancied that she blushed.

"Aha," said Mr. Satterthwaite to himself. "Let's see how you get out of this, young lady."

"It was silly of me," said Egg. "I got confused. I thought

89

that Oliver, arriving as he did, with what might have been a trumped-up excuse—well, I thought the police were sure to suspect him."

Sir Charles accepted the explanation easily enough.

"Yes," he said. "I see."

Mr. Satterthwaite spoke.

"Was it a trumped-up excuse?" he said.

Egg turned on him.

"What do you mean?"

"It was an odd sort of accident," said Mr. Satterthwaite. "I thought if it was a trumped-up excuse, you might know."

Egg shook her head.

"I don't know. I never thought about it. But why should Oliver pretend to have an accident if he didn't?"

"He might have had reasons," said Sir Charles. "Quite natural ones."

He was smiling at her. Egg blushed crimson.

"Oh, no," she said. "No."

Sir Charles sighed. It occurred to Mr. Satterthwaite that his friend had interpreted that blush quite wrongly. Sir Charles seemed a sadder and older man when he spoke again.

"Well," he said, "if our young friend Manders is in no danger, where do I come in?"

Egg came forward quickly and caught him by the coat sleeve.

"You're not going away again. You're not going to give up. You're going to find out the truth—the truth. I don't believe anybody but you could find out the truth. You can. You will."

She was tremendously in earnest. The waves of her vitality seemed to surge and eddy in the Old World air of the room.

"You believe in me?" said Sir Charles. He was moved.

"Yes, yes, yes. We're going to get at the truth. You and I together."

"And Satterthwaite."

"Of course, and Mr. Satterthwaite," said Egg without interest.

Mr. Satterthwaite smiled covertly. Whether Egg wanted to include him or not, he had no intention of being left out. He was fond of mysteries, and he liked observing human nature, and he had a soft spot for lovers. All three tastes seemed likely to be gratified in this affair.

Sir Charles sat down. His voice changed. He was in command, directing a production.

"First of all, we've got to clarify the situation. Do we, or do we not, believe that the same person killed Babbington and Bartholomew Strange?"

"Yes," said Egg.

"Yes," said Mr. Satterthwaite.

"Do we believe that the second murder sprang directly from the first? I mean, do we believe that Bartholomew Strange was killed in order to prevent his revealing the facts of the first murder, or his suspicion about it?"

"Yes," said Egg and Mr. Satterthwaite again, but in unison this time.

"Then it is the first murder we must investigate, not the second."

Egg nodded.

"In my mind, until we discover the motive for the first murder, we can hardly hope to discover the murderer. The motive presents extraordinary difficulty. Babbington was a harmless, pleasant, gentle old man without, one would say, an enemy in the world. Yet he was killed, and there must have been some reason for the killing. We've got to find that reason."

He paused and then said in his ordinary everyday voice:

"Let's get down to it. What reasons are there for killing people? First, I suppose, gain."

"Revenge," said Egg.

"Homicidal mania," said Mr. Satterthwaite. "The *crime passionnel* would hardly apply in this case. But there's fear."

Charles Cartwright nodded. He was scribbling on a piece of paper.

"That about covers the ground," he said. "First: Gain. Does anyone gain by Babbington's death? Has he any money, or any expectations of money?"

"I should think it very unlikely," said Egg.

"So should I, but we'd better approach Mrs. Babbington on the point."

"Then there's revenge. Did Babbington do any injury to anyone—perhaps in his young days? Did he marry the girl that some other man wanted? We'll have to look into that too.

"Then homicidal mania. Both Babbington and Tollie were killed by a lunatic. I don't think that theory will hold water.

91

Even a lunatic has some kind of reasonableness in his crimes. I mean a lunatic might think himself divinely appointed to kill doctors or to kill clergymen, but not to kill both. I think we can wash out the theory of homicidal mania. There remains fear.

"Now, frankly, that seems to me far the most likely solution. Babbington knew something about somebody, or he recognized somebody. He was killed to prevent him telling what that something was."

"I can't see what someone like Mr. Babbington could know that was damaging about anybody who was there that night."

"Perhaps," said Sir Charles, "it was something that he didn't know that he knew."

He went on, trying to make his meaning clear:

"It's difficult to say just what I mean. Suppose, for instance—this is only an instance—that Babbington saw a certain person in a certain place at a certain time. As far as he knows, there's no reason why that person shouldn't be there. But suppose, also, that that person had concocted a very clever alibi for some reason, showing that at that particular time he was somewhere else a hundred miles away. Well, at any minute old Babbington, in the most innocent way in the world, might give the show away."

"I see," said Egg. "Say there's a murder committed in London, and Babbington sees the man who did it at Paddington Station, but the man has proved that he didn't do it by having an alibi showing that he was at Leeds at the time. Then Babbington might give the whole show away."

"That's what I mean exactly. Of course, that's only an instance. It might be anything. Someone he saw that evening whom he'd known under a different name."

"It might be something to do with a marriage," said Egg. "Clergymen do lots of marriages. Somebody who'd committed bigamy."

"Or it might have to do with a birth or a death," suggested Mr. Satterthwaite.

"It's a very wide field," said Egg, frowning. "We'll have to get at it the other way. Work back from the people who were there. Let's make a list. Who was at your house and who was at Sir Bartholomew's?"

She took the paper and pencil from Sir Charles.

"The Dacreses, they were at both. That woman like a wilted cabbage—what's her name?—Wills. Miss Sutcliffe."

"You can leave Angela out of it," said Sir Charles. "I've known her for years."

Egg frowned mutinously.

"We can't do that sort of thing," she said. "Leave people out because we know them. We've got to be businesslike. Besides, I don't know anything about Angela Sutcliffe. She's just as likely to have done it as anyone else, so far as I can see—more likely. All actresses have pasts. I think, on the whole, she's the most likely person."

She gazed defiantly at Sir Charles. There was an answering spark in his eyes.

"In that case, we mustn't leave out Oliver Manders."

"How could it be Oliver? He'd met Mr. Babbington ever so many times before."

"He was at both places, and his arrival is a little open to suspicion."

"Very well," said Egg. She paused, and then added: "In that case, I'd better put down mother and myself as well. That makes seven suspects."

"I don't think——"

"We'll do it properly, or not at all." Her eyes flashed.

Mr. Satterthwaite made peace by offering refreshment. He rang for drinks.

Sir Charles strolled off into a far corner to admire a head of negro sculpture. Egg came over to Mr. Satterthwaite and slipped a hand through his arm.

"Stupid of me to have lost my temper," she murmured. "I am stupid—but why should the woman be excepted? Why is he so keen she should be? Oh, dear, why the devil am I so disgustingly jealous?"

Mr. Satterthwaite smiled and patted her hand.

"Jealousy never pays, my dear," he said. "If you feel jealous, don't show it. By the way, did you really think that young Manders might be suspected?"

Egg grinned—a friendly, childish grin.

"Of course not. I put that in so as not to alarm the man." She turned her head. Sir Charles was still moodily studying negro sculpture. "You know, I didn't want him to think I really have a pash for Oliver, because I haven't. How difficult everything is! He's gone back now to his 'Bless you, my children' attitude. I don't want that at all."

"Have patience," counseled Mr. Satterthwaite. "Everything comes right in the end, you know."

"I'm not patient," said Egg. "I want to have things at once or even quicker."

Mr. Satterthwaite laughed, and Sir Charles turned and came toward them.

As they sipped their drinks, they arranged a plan of campaign. Sir Charles should return to Crow's Nest, for which he had not yet found a purchaser. Egg and her mother would return to Rose Cottage rather sooner than they had meant to do. Mrs. Babbington was still living in Loomouth. They would get what information they could from her and then proceed to act upon it.

"We'll succeed," said Egg. "I know we'll succeed."

She leaned forward to Sir Charles, her eyes glowing. She held out her glass to touch his.

"Drink to our success," she commanded.

Slowly, very slowly, his eyes fixed on hers, he raised his glass to his lips.

"To success," he said, "and to the future."

THIRD ACT

DISCOVERY

CHAPTER XIII

Mrs. Babbington had moved into a small fisherman's cottage not far from the harbor. She was expecting a sister home from Japan in about six months. Until her sister arrived, she was making no plans for the future. The cottage chanced to be vacant and she took it for six months. She felt too bewildered by her sudden loss to move away from Loomouth. Stephen Babbington had held the living of St. Petroch, Loomouth, for seventeen years. They had been, on the whole, seventeen happy and peaceful years, in spite of the sorrow occasioned by the death of her son Robin. Of her remaining children, Edward was in Ceylon, Lloyd was in South Africa, and Stephen was third officer on the *Angolia*. They wrote frequently and affectionately, but they could offer neither a home nor companionship to their mother.

Margaret Babbington was very lonely.

Not that she allowed herself much time for thinking. She was still active in the parish—the new vicar was unmarried—and she spent a good deal of time working in the tiny plot of ground in front of the cottage. She was a woman whose flowers were part of her life.

She was working there one afternoon, when she heard the latch of the gate click, and looked up to see Sir Charles Cartwright and Egg Lytton Gore.

Margaret was not surprised to see Egg. She knew that the girl and her mother were due to return shortly. But she was surprised to see Sir Charles. Rumor had insisted that he had left the neighborhood for good. There had been paragraphs copied from other papers about his doings in the South of

France. There had been a board, TO BE SOLD, stuck up in the garden of Crow's Nest. No one had expected Sir Charles to return. Yet return he had.

Mrs. Babbington shook the untidy hair back from her hot forehead and looked ruefully at her earthstained hands.

"I'm not fit to shake hands," she said. "I ought to garden in gloves, I know. I do start in them sometimes. But I always tear them off sooner or later. One can feel things so much better with bare hands."

She led the way into the house. The tiny sitting room had been made cozy with chintz. There were photographs and bowls of chrysanthemums.

"It's a great surprise seeing you, Sir Charles. I thought you had given up Crow's Nest for good."

"I thought I had," said the actor frankly. "But sometimes, Mrs. Babbington, our destiny is too strong for us."

Mrs. Babbington did not reply. She turned toward Egg, but the girl forestalled the words on her lips.

"Look here, Mrs. Babbington. This isn't just a call. Sir Charles and I have got something very serious to say. Only I—I should hate to upset you."

Mrs. Babbington looked from the girl to Sir Charles. Her face had gone rather gray and pinched.

"First of all," said Sir Charles, "I would like to ask you if you have had any communication from the Home Office?"

Mrs. Babbington bowed her head.

"I see. Well, perhaps that makes what we are about to say easier."

"Is that what you have come about—this exhumation order?"

"Yes. It is—I'm afraid it must be—very distressing to you?"

She softened to the sympathy in his voice.

"Perhaps I do not mind as much as you think. To some people, the idea of exhumation is very dreadful; not to me. It is not the dead clay that matters. My dear husband is elsewhere, at peace—where no one can trouble his rest. No, it is not that. It is the idea that is a shock to me—the idea—a terrible one—that Stephen did not die a natural death. It seems so impossible—utterly impossible."

"I'm afraid it must seem so to you. It did to me—to us—at first."

98

"What do you mean by 'at first,' Sir Charles?"

"Because the suspicion crossed my mind on the evening of your husband's death, Mrs. Babbington. Like you, however, it seemed to me so impossible that I put it aside."

"I thought so too," said Egg.

"You too?" Mrs. Babbington looked at her wonderingly. "You thought someone could have killed—Stephen?"

The incredulity in her voice was so great that neither of her visitors knew quite how to proceed. At last Sir Charles took up the tale:

"As you know, Mrs. Babbington, I went abroad. When I was in the South of France I read in the paper of my friend Bartholomew Strange's death in almost exactly similar circumstances. I also got a letter from Miss Lytton Gore."

Egg nodded.

"I was there, you know, staying with him at the time. Mrs. Babbington, it was exactly the same—exactly. He drank some port and his face changed and—and—well, it was just the same. He died two or three minutes later."

Mrs. Babbington shook her head slowly.

"I can't understand it. Stephen! Sir Bartholomew—a kind and clever doctor! Who could want to harm either of them? It must be a mistake."

"Sir Bartholomew was proved to have been poisoned, remember," said Sir Charles.

"Then it must have been the work of a lunatic."

Sir Charles went on:

"Mrs. Babbington, I want to get to the bottom of this. I want to find out the truth. And I feel there is no time to lose. Once the news of the exhumation gets about, our criminal will be on the alert. I am assuming, for the sake of saving time, what the result of the autopsy on your husband's body will be. I am taking it that he, too, died of nicotine poisoning. To begin with, did you or he know anything about the use of pure nicotine?"

"I always use a solution of nicotine for spraying roses. I didn't know it was supposed to be poisonous."

"I should imagine—I was reading up on the subject last night—that in both cases the pure alkaloid must have been used. Cases of poisoning by nicotine are most unusual."

Mrs. Babbington shook her head.

"I really don't know anything about nicotine poisoning, except that I suppose inveterate smokers might suffer from it."

"Did your husband smoke?"

"Yes."

"Now tell me, Mrs. Babbington. You have expressed the utmost surprise that anyone should want to do away with your husband. Does that mean that, as far as you know, he had no enemies?"

"I am sure Stephen had no emenies. Everyone was fond of him. People tried to hustle him sometimes." She smiled a little tearfully. "He was getting on, you know, and rather afraid of innovations, but everybody liked him. You couldn't dislike Stephen, Sir Charles."

"I suppose, Mrs. Babbington, that your husband didn't leave very much money?"

"No. Next to nothing. Stephen was not good at saving. He gave away far too much. I used to scold him about it."

"I suppose he had no expectations from anyone? He wasn't the heir to any property?"

"Oh, no. Stephen hadn't many relations. He has a sister who is married to a clergyman in Northumberland, but they are very badly off, and all his uncles and aunts are dead."

"Then it does not seem as though there were anyone who could benefit by Mr. Babbington's death."

"No, indeed."

"Let us come back to the question of enemies for a minute. Your husband had no enemies, you say, but he may have had as a young man."

Mrs. Babbington looked skeptical.

"I should think it very unlikely. Stephen hadn't a quarrelsome nature. He always got on well with people."

"I don't want to sound melodramatic"—Sir Charles coughed a little nervously—"but—er—when he got engaged to you, for instance, there wasn't any disappointed suitor in the offing?"

A momentary twinkle came into Mrs. Babbington's eyes.

"Stephen was my father's curate. He was the first young man I saw when I came home from school. I fell in love with him and he with me. We were engaged for four years and then he got a living down in Kent and we were able to get

100

married. Ours was a very simple love story, Sir Charles, and a very happy one."

Sir Charles bowed his head. Mrs. Babbington's simple dignity was very charming.

Egg took up the role of questioner:

"Mrs. Babbington, do you think your husband had met any of the guests at Sir Charles's that night before?"

Mrs. Babbington looked slightly puzzled.

"Well, there were you and your mother, my dear, and young Oliver Manders."

"Yes, but any of the others?"

"We had both seen Angela Sutcliffe in a play in London five years ago. Both Stephen and I were very excited that we were actually going to meet her."

"You had never actually met her before?"

"No. We've never met any actresses—or actors, for the matter of that—until Sir Charles came to live here. And that," added Mrs. Babbington, "was a great excitement. I don't think Sir Charles knows what a wonderful thing it was to us. Quite a breath of romance in our lives."

"You hadn't met Captain and Mrs. Dacres?"

"Was he the little man with the woman with the wonderful clothes?"

"Yes."

"No. Nor the other woman—the one who wrote plays. Poor thing, she looked rather out of it, I thought."

"You're sure you'd never seen any of them before?"

"I'm quite sure I hadn't, and so I'm fairly sure Stephen hadn't either. You see, we do everything together."

"And Mr. Babbington didn't say anything to you—anything at all," persisted Egg—"about the people you were going to meet, or about them when he saw them?"

"Nothing beforehand, except that he was looking forward to an interesting evening. And when we got there—well, there wasn't much time——" Her face twisted suddenly.

Sir Charles broke in quickly:

"You must forgive us badgering you like this. But, you see, we feel that there must be something, if only we could get at it. There must be some reason for an apparently brutal and meaningless murder."

"I see that," said Mrs. Babbington. "If it was murder,

there must be some reason. But I don't know—I can't imagine—what the reason could be."

There was silence for a minute or two, then Sir Charles said:

"Can you give me a slight biographical sketch of your husband's career?"

Mrs. Babbington had a good memory for dates, as Sir Charles's final notes disclosed.

Stephen Babbington, born Islington, Devon, 1868. Educated St. Paul's School and Oxford. Ordained deacon and received a title to the parish of Hoxton, 1891. Priested 1892. Was curate of Elsington, Surrey, to Rev. Vernon Lorrimer 1894–1899. Married Margaret Lorrimer, 1899, and presented to the living of St. Mary's, Gilling. Transferred to living of St. Petroch, Loomouth, 1916.

"That gives us something to go upon," said Sir Charles. "Our best chance seems to me the time during which Mr. Babbington was vicar of St. Mary's, Gilling. His earlier history seems rather far back to concern any of the people who were at my house that evening."

Mrs. Babbington shuddered.

"Do you really think that one of them——"

"I don't know what to think," said Sir Charles. "Bartholomew Strange saw something or guessed something, and Bartholomew Strange died the same way, and five——"

"Seven," said Egg.

"——of these people were also present. One of them must be guilty."

"But why?" cried Mrs. Babbington. "Why? What possible motive could there be for anyone to want to kill Stephen?"

"That," said Sir Charles, "is what we are going to find out."

CHAPTER XIV

M R. Satterthwaite had come down to Crow's Nest with Sir Charles. While his host and Egg Lytton Gore were visiting Mrs. Babbington, Mr. Satterthwaite was having tea with Lady Mary.

Lady Mary liked Mr. Satterthwaite. For all her gentleness of manner, she was a woman who had very definite views on the subject of whom she did or did not like.

Mr. Satterthwaite sipped China tea from a Dresden cup, and ate a microscopic sandwich and chatted. On his last visit, they had found many friends and acquaintances in common. Their talk today began on the same subject, but gradually drifted into more intimate channels. Mr. Satterthwaite was a sympathetic person; he listened to the troubles of other people and did not intrude his own. Even on his last visit, it had seemed natural to Lady Mary to speak to him of her preoccupation with her daughter's future. She talked now as she would have talked to a friend of many years' standing.

"Egg is so headstrong," she said. "She flings herself into a thing heart and soul. You know, Mr. Satterthwaite, I do not like the way she is—well, mixing herself up in this distressing business. It—Egg would laugh at me, I know—but it doesn't seem to be ladylike."

She flushed as she spoke. Her brown eyes, gentle and ingenuous, looked with a childish appeal at Mr. Satterthwaite.

"I know what you mean," he said. "I confess that I don't quite like it myself. I know that it's simply an old-fashioned prejudice, but there it is. All the same"—he twinkled at her—"we can't expect young ladies to sit at home and sew

103

and shudder at the idea of crimes of violence in these enlightened days."

"I don't like to think of murder," said Lady Mary. "I never, never dreamed that I should be mixed up in anything of that kind. It was dreadful." She shivered. "Poor Sir Bartholomew."

"You didn't know him very well?" hazarded Mr. Satterthwaite.

"I think I'd only met him twice. The first time about a year ago, when he came down to stay with Sir Charles for a week-end, and the second time was on that dreadful evening when poor Mr. Babbington died. I was really most surprised when his invitation arrived. I accepted because I thought Egg would enjoy it. She hasn't many treats, poor child, and—well, she had seemed a little down in the mouth—as though she didn't take any interest in anything. I thought a big house party might cheer her up."

Mr. Satterthwaite nodded.

"Tell me something about young Oliver Manders," he said. "The young fellow rather interests me."

"I think he's clever," said Lady Mary. "Of course, things have been difficult for him."

She flushed, and then, in answer to the plain inquiry of Mr. Satterthwaite's glance, she went on:

"You see, his father wasn't married to his mother."

"Really? I had no idea of that."

"Everyone knows about it down here, otherwise I wouldn't have said anything about it. Old Mrs. Manders, Oliver's grandmother, lives at Dunboyne, that biggish house on the Plymouth road. Her husband was a lawyer down there. Her son went into a city firm and did very well. He's quite a rich man. The daughter was a good-looking girl and she became absolutely infatuated with a married man. I blame him very much indeed. Anyway, in the end, after a lot of scandal, they went off together. His wife wouldn't divorce him. The girl died not long after Oliver was born. His uncle in London took charge of him. He and his wife had no children of their own. The boy divided his time between them and his grandmother. He always came down here for his summer holidays."

She paused and then went on:

"I always felt sorry for him. I still do. I think that terribly conceited manner of his is a good deal put on."

"I shouldn't be surprised," said Mr. Satterthwaite. "It's a very common phenomenon. If I ever see anyone who appears to think only of himself and boasts unceasingly, I always know that there's a secret sense of inferiority somewhere."

"It seems very odd."

"An inferiority complex is a very peculiar thing. Crippen, for instance, undoubtedly suffered from it. It's at the back of a lot of crimes. The desire to assert one's personality."

"It seems very strange to me," murmured Lady Mary.

She seemed to shrink a little. Mr. Satterthwaite looked at her with an almost sentimental eye. He liked her graceful figure with the sloping shoulders, the soft brown of her eyes, her complete absence of make-up. He thought:

"She must have been a beauty when she was young."

Not a flaunting beauty, not a rose; no, a modest, charming violet, hiding its sweetness.

His thoughts ran serenely in the idiom of his young days.

He remembered incidents in his own youth.

Presently he found himself telling Lady Mary about his own love affair—the only love affair he had ever had. Rather a poor love affair by the standards of today, but very dear to Mr. Satterthwaite.

He told her about the girl and how pretty she was, and of how they had gone together to see the bluebells at Kew. He had meant to propose to her that day. He had imagined—so he put it—that she reciprocated his sentiments. And then, as they were standing looking at the bluebells, she had confided in him. He had discovered that she loved another. And he had hidden the thoughts surging in his breast and had taken up the rôle of the faithful friend.

It was not, perhaps, a very full-blooded romance, but it sounded well in the dim faded chintz and eggshell china atmosphere of Lady Mary's drawing-room.

Afterward, Lady Mary spoke of her own life—of her married life, which had not been very happy.

"I was such a foolish girl—girls are foolish, Mr. Satterthwaite. They are so sure of themselves, so convinced they know best. People write and talk a lot of a woman's instinct. I don't believe, Mr. Satterthwaite, that there is any such thing.

Their parents warn them, but that's no good; one doesn't believe. It seems dreadful to say so, but there is something attractive to a girl in being told anyone is a bad man. She thinks at once that her love will reform him."

Mr. Satterthwaite nodded gently.

"One knows so little. When one knows more, it is too late."

She sighed.

"It was all my own fault. My people didn't want me to marry Ronald. He was well-born, but he had a bad reputation. My father told me straight out that he was a wrong un. I didn't believe it; I believed that, for my sake, he would turn over a new leaf."

She was silent a moment, dwelling on the past.

"Ronald was a very fascinating man. My father was quite right about him. I soon found that out. It's an old-fashioned thing to say, but he broke my heart. Yes, he broke my heart. I was always afraid of what might come out next."

Mr. Satterthwaite, always intensely interested in other people's lives, made a cautious sympathetic noise.

"It may seem a very wicked thing to say, Mr. Satterthwaite, but it was a relief when he got pneumonia and died. Not that I didn't care for him—I loved him up to the end—but I had no illusions about him any longer. And there was Egg."

Her voice softened:

"Such a funny little thing, she was. A regular little roly-poly, trying to stand up and falling over. Just like an egg—that's how that ridiculous nickname started."

She paused again.

"Some books that I've read these last few years have brought a lot of comfort to me. Books on psychology. It seems to show that in many ways people can't help themselves. A kind of kink. Sometimes, in the most carefully brought-up families, you get it. As a boy, Ronald stole money at school—money that he didn't need. I can feel now that he couldn't help himself. He was born with a kink."

Very gently, with a small handkerchief, Lady Mary wiped her eyes.

"It wasn't what I was brought up to believe," she said apologetically. "I was taught that everyone knew the differ-

106

ence between right and wrong. But somehow, I don't always think that is so."

"The human mind is a great mystery," said Mr. Satterthwaite gently. "As yet, we are only groping our way to understanding. Without acute mania, it may nevertheless occur that certain natures lack what I should describe as braking power. If you or I were to say, 'I hate someone; I wish he were dead,' the idea would pass from our minds as soon as the words were uttered. The brakes would work automatically. But in some people the idea, or obsession, holds. They see nothing but the immediate gratification of the idea formed."

"I'm afraid," said Lady Mary, "that that's rather too clever for me."

"I apologize. I was talking rather bookishly."

"Did you mean that young people have too little restraint nowadays?"

"No, no, I didn't mean that at all. Less restraint is, I think, a good thing—wholesome. I suppose you are thinking of Miss—er—Egg."

"I think you'd better call her Egg," said Lady Mary, smiling.

"Thank you. Miss Egg does sound rather ridiculous."

"Egg's very impulsive and once she has set her mind on a thing, nothing will stop her. As I said before, I hate her mixing herself up in all this, but she won't listen to me."

Mr. Satterthwaite smiled at the distress in Lady Mary's tone. He thought to himself:

"I wonder if she realizes for one minute that Egg's absorption in crime is neither more nor less than a new variant of that old, old game, the pursuit of the male by the female. No, Lady Mary would be horrified at the thought."

"Egg says that Mr. Babbington was poisoned also. Do you think that is true, Mr. Satterthwaite? Or do you think it is just one of Egg's sweeping statements?"

"We shall know for certain after the exhumation."

"There is to be an exhumation, then?" Lady Mary shivered. "How terrible for poor Mrs. Babbington! I can imagine nothing more awful for any woman."

"You knew the Babbingtons fairly intimately, I suppose, Lady Mary?"

"Yes, indeed. They are—were—very dear friends of ours."

"Do you know of anyone who could possibly have had a grudge against the vicar?"

"No, indeed."

"He never spoke to you of such a person?"

"No."

"And the Babbingtons got on well together?"

"They were perfectly mated—happy in each other and in their children. They were badly off, of course, and Mr. Babbington suffered from rheumatoid arthritis. Those were their only troubles."

"How did Oliver Manders get on with the vicar?"

"Well——" Lady Mary hesitated. "They didn't hit it off very well. The Babbingtons were sorry for Oliver and he used to go to the vicarage a good deal on the holidays to play with the Babbington boys; though I don't think he got on very well with them. Oliver wasn't exactly a popular boy. He boasted too much of the money he had, and the tuck he took back to school and all the fun he had in London. Boys are rather merciless about that sort of thing."

"Yes, but later—since he's been grown up."

"I don't think he and the vicarage people have seen much of each other. As a matter of fact, Oliver was rather rude to Mr. Babbington one day here in my house. It was about two years ago."

"What happened?"

"Oliver made a rather ill-bred attack on Christianity. Mr. Babbington was very patient and courteous with him. That only seemed to make Oliver worse. He said: 'All you religious people look down your noses because my father and mother weren't married. I suppose you'd call me the child of sin. Well, I admire people who have the courage of their convictions and don't care what a lot of hypocrites and parsons think.' Mr. Babbington didn't answer, but Oliver went on: 'You won't answer that. It's ecclesiasticism and superstition that's got the whole world into the mess it's in. I'd like to sweep away the churches all over the world.' Mr. Babbington smiled and said, 'And the clergy too?' I think it was his smile that annoyed Oliver. He felt he wasn't being taken seriously. He said, 'I hate everything the church stands for. Smugness, security and hypocrisy. Get rid of the whole canting tribe, I say.' And Mr. Babbington smiled—he had a very sweet smile—

and he said, 'My dear boy, if you were to sweep away all the churches ever built or planned, you would still have to reckon with God.' "

"What did young Manders say to that?"

"He seemed taken aback, and then he recovered his temper and went back to his usual sneering, tired manner.

"He said, 'I'm afraid the things I've been saying are rather bad form, padre, and not very easily assimilated by your generation.' "

"You don't like young Manders, do you, Lady Mary?"

"I'm sorry for him," said Lady Mary defensively.

"But you wouldn't like him to marry Egg."

"Oh, no."

"I wonder why exactly."

"Because—because he isn't kind. And because——"

"Yes?"

"Because there's something in him somewhere that I don't understand. Something cold."

Mr. Satterthwaite looked at her thoughtfully for a minute or two, then he said:

"What did Sir Bartholomew Strange think of him? Did he ever mention him?"

"He said, I remember, that he found young Manders an interesting study. He said that he reminded him of a case he was treating at the moment in his nursing home. I said that I thought Oliver looked particularly strong and healthy, and he said, 'Yes, his health's all right, but he's riding for a fall.' "

She paused, and then said:

"I suppose Sir Bartholomew was a very clever doctor."

"I believe he was very highly thought of by his own colleagues."

"I liked him," said Lady Mary.

"Did he ever say anything to you about Babbington's death?"

"No."

"He never mentioned it at all?"

"I don't think so."

"Do you think—it's difficult for you to tell, not knowing him well—but do you think he had anything on his mind?"

"He seemed in very good spirits; even amused by something—some private joke of his own. He told me at dinner that night that he was going to spring a surprise on me."

"Oh, he did, did he?"

On his way home, Mr. Satterthwaite pondered that statement.

What had been the surprise Sir Bartholomew had intended to spring on his guests?

Would it, when it came, have been as amusing as he pretended?

Or did that gay manner mask a quiet but indomitable purpose? Would anyone ever know?

CHAPTER XV

"**F**RANKLY," said Sir Charles, "are we any forrader?"

It was a council of war. Sir Charles, Mr. Satterthwaite and Egg Lytton Gore were sitting in the ship room. A fire burned in the grate and outside an equinoctial gale was howling.

Mr. Satterthwaite and Egg answered the question simultaneously.

"No," said Mr. Satterthwaite.

"Yes," said Egg.

Sir Charles looked from one to the other of them. Mr. Satterthwaite indicated gracefully that the lady should speak first.

Egg was silent a moment or two, collecting her ideas.

"We are further on," she said at last. "We are further on because we haven't found out anything. That sounds nonsense, but it isn't. What I mean is we had certain vague, sketchy ideas; we know now that certain of those ideas are definitely washouts."

"Progress by elimination," said Sir Charles.

"That's it."

Mr. Satterthwaite cleared his throat.

"The idea of gain we can now put definitely away," he said. "There does not seem to be anybody who, in detective-story parlance, could 'benefit by Stephen Babbington's death.' Revenge seems equally out of the question. Apart from his naturally amiable and peace-loving disposition, I doubt if he were important enough to make enemies. So we are back at

111

our last rather sketchy idea. Fear. By the death of Stephen Babbington, someone gains security."

"That's rather well put," said Egg.

Mr. Satterthwaite looked modestly pleased with himself. Sir Charles looked a little annoyed. His was the star part, not Satterthwaite's.

"The point is," said Egg: "What are we going to do next—actually do, I mean? Are we going to sleuth people, or what? Are we going to disguise ourselves and follow them?"

"My dear child," said Sir Charles, "I always did set my face against playing old men in beards, and I'm not going to begin now."

"Then what——" began Egg.

But she was interrupted. The door opened and Temple announced:

"M. Hercule Poirot."

M. Poirot walked in with a beaming face and greeted three highly astonished people.

"It is permitted," he said with a twinkle, "that I assist at this conference? I am right, am I not? It is a conference?"

"My dear fellow, we're delighted to see you." Sir Charles, recovering from his surprise, shook his guest warmly by the hand and pushed him into a large armchair. "Where have you sprung from so suddenly?"

"I went to call upon my good friend Mr. Satterthwaite in London. They tell me he is away—in Cornwall. *Eh bien,* it leaps to the eye where he has gone. I take the first train to Loomouth and here I am."

"Yes," said Egg, "but why have you come? I mean," she went on, blushing a little as she realized the possible discourtesy of her words, "you have come for some particular reason."

"I have come," said Hercule Poirot, "to admit an error."

With an engaging smile he turned to Sir Charles and spread out his hands in a foreign gesture.

"Monsieur, it was in this very room that you declared yourself not satisfied. And I—I thought it was your dramatic instinct—I said to myself, 'He is a great actor; at all costs he must have drama.' It seemed—I will admit it—incredible that a harmless old gentleman should have died of anything but a

natural death. Even now I do not see how poison could have
been administered to him, nor can I guess at any motive. It
seems absurd—fantastic. And yet, since then, there has been
another death—a death under such similar circumstances
that one cannot attribute it to coincidence. No, there must be
a link between the two. And so, Sir Charles, I have come to
you to apologize—to say, I, Hercule Poirot, was wrong, and to
ask you to admit me to your councils."

Sir Charles cleared his throat rather nervously. He looked
a little embarrassed.

"That's extraordinarily handsome of you, M. Poirot. I
don't know—taking up a lot of your time—I——"

He stopped, somewhat at a loss. His eyes consulted Mr.
Satterthwaite.

"It is very good of you——" began Mr. Satterthwaite.

"No, no, it is not good of me. It is the curiosity, and—yes,
the hurt to my pride. I must repair my fault. My time—that
is nothing. Why voyage after all? The language may be different, but everywhere human nature is the same. But of course
if I am not welcome, if you feel that I intrude——"

Both men spoke at once:

"No, indeed."

"Rather not."

Poirot turned his eyes to the girl.

"And mademoiselle?"

For a minute or two, Egg was silent, and on all three men
the same impression was produced: Egg did not want the
assistance of M. Poirot.

Mr. Satterthwaite thought he knew why. This was the
private play of Charles Cartwright and Egg Lytton Gore. Mr.
Satterthwaite had been admitted on sufferance—on the clear
understanding that he was a negligible third party. But Hercule
Poirot was different. His would be the leading role. Perhaps,
even, Sir Charles might retire in his favor. And then Egg's
plans would come to naught.

He watched the girl, sympathizing with her predicament.
These men did not understand, but he, with his semi-feminine
sensitiveness, realized her dilemma. Egg was fighting for her
happiness.

What would she say?

After all, what could she say? How could she speak the thoughts in her mind? "Go away—go away; your coming may spoil everything. I don't want you here."

Egg Lytton Gore said the only thing she could say.

"Of course," she said, with a little smile, "we'd love to have you."

CHAPTER XVI

"GOOD," said Poirot. "We are colleagues. *Eh bien,* you will put me, if you please, *au courant* of the situation."

He listened with close attention whilst Mr. Satterthwaite outlined the steps they had taken since returning to England. Mr. Satterthwaite was a good narrator. He had the faculty of creating an atmosphere, of painting a picture. His description of the abbey, of the servants, of the chief constable, was admirable. Poirot was warm in his appreciation of the discovery by Sir Charles of the unfinished letters under the gas fire.

"*Ah, mais c'est magnifique, ça!*" he exclaimed ecstatically. "The deduction, the reconstruction—perfect! You should have been a great detective, Sir Charles, instead of a great actor."

Sir Charles received these plaudits with becoming modesty —his own particular brand of modesty. He had not received compliments on his stage performances for many years without perfecting a manner of acknowledging them.

"Your observation, too, it was very just," said Poirot, turning to Mr. Satterthwaite. "That point of yours about his sudden familiarity with the butler."

"Do you think there is anything in this Mrs. de Rush-bridger idea?" asked Sir Charles eagerly.

"It is an idea. It suggests—well, it suggests several things, does it not?"

Nobody was quite sure about the several things, but nobody liked to say so, so there was merely an assenting murmur.

Sir Charles took up the tale next. He described his and Egg's visit to Mrs. Babbington and its rather negative result.

"And now you're up to date," he said. "You know what we do. Tell us, how does it all strike you?"

115

He leaned forward, boyishly eager.

Poirot was silent for some minutes. The other three watched him.

He said at last:

"Can you remember at all, mademoiselle, what type of port glass Sir Bartholomew had on his table?"

Sir Charles interposed just as Egg was shaking her head vexedly.

"I can tell you that."

He got up and went to a cupboard, where he took out some heavy cut-glass sherry glasses.

"They were a slightly different shape, of course—more rounded—proper port shape. He got them at old Lammersfield's sale—a whole set of table glass. I admired them, and as there were more than he needed, he passed some of them on to me. They're good, aren't they?"

Poirot took the glass and turned it about in his hand.

"Yes," he said. "They are fine specimens. I thought something of that kind had been used."

"Why?" cried Egg.

Poirot merely smiled at her.

"Yes," he went on, "the death of Sir Bartholomew Strange could be explained easily enough, but the death of Stephen Babbington is more difficult. Ah, if only it had been the other way about!"

"What do you mean—the other way about?" asked Mr. Satterthwaite.

Poirot turned to him.

"Consider, my friend. Sir Bartholomew is a celebrated doctor. There might be many reasons for the death of a celebrated doctor. A doctor knows secrets, my friend—important secrets. A doctor has certain powers. Imagine a patient on the border line of sanity. A word from the doctor and he will be shut away from the world; what a temptation to an unbalanced brain. A doctor may have suspicions about the sudden death of one of his patients. Oh, yes, we can find plenty of motives for the death of a doctor.

"Now, as I say, if only it had been the other way about. If Sir Bartholomew Strange had died first and then Stephen Babbington. For Stephen Babbington might have seen something—might have suspected something about the first death."

He sighed and then resumed:

"But one cannot have a case as one would like to have it. One must take a case as it is. Just one little idea I should like to suggest. I suppose it is not possible that Stephen Babbington's death was an accident—that the poison—if poison there was—was intended for Sir Bartholomew Strange, and that, by mistake, the wrong man was killed."

"That's an ingenious idea," said Sir Charles. His face, which had brightened, fell again. "But I don't believe it will work. Babbington came into this room about four minutes before he was taken ill. During that time the only thing that passed his lips was half a cocktail; there was nothing in that cocktail——"

Poirot interrupted him:

"That, you have already told me, but suppose, for the sake of argument, that there was something in that cocktail. Could it have been intended for Sir Bartholomew Strange and did Mr. Babbington drink it by mistake?"

Sir Charles shook his head.

"Nobody who knew Tollie at all well would have tried poisoning him in a cocktail."

"Why?"

"Because he never drank them."

"Never?"

"Never."

Poirot made a gesture of annoyance.

"Ah, this business: it goes all wrong. It does not make sense."

"Besides," went on Sir Charles, "I don't see how any one glass could have been mistaken for another, or anything of that kind. Temple carried them round on a tray and everyone helped themselves to any glass they fancied."

"True," murmured Poirot. "One cannot force a cocktail like one forces a card. What is she like, this Temple of yours? She is the maid who admitted me tonight, yes?"

"That's right. I've had her three or four years—nice steady girl, knows her work. I don't know where she came from. Miss Milray would know all about that."

"Miss Milray—that is your secretary? The tall woman, somewhat of the grenadier?"

"Very much of the grenadier," agreed Sir Charles.

"I have dined with you before on various occasions, but I do not think I met her until that night."

"No, she doesn't usually dine with us. It was a question of thirteen, you see."

Sir Charles explained the circumstances, to which Poirot listened very attentively.

"It was her own suggestion that she should be present. I see."

He remained lost in thought a minute, then he said:

"Might I speak to this parlormaid of yours—this Temple?"

"Certainly, my dear fellow."

Sir Charles pressed a bell. It was answered promptly:

"You rang, sir?"

Temple was a tall girl of thirty-two or three. She had a certain smartness; her hair was well brushed and glossy, but she was not pretty. Her manner was calm and efficient.

"M. Poirot wants to ask you a few questions," said Sir Charles.

Temple transferred her superior gaze to Poirot.

"We are talking of the night when Mr. Babbington died here," said Poirot. "You remember that night?"

"Oh, yes, sir."

"I want to know exactly how the cocktails were served."

"I beg your pardon, sir."

"I want to know about the cocktails. Did you mix them?"

"No, sir, Sir Charles likes doing that himself. I brought in the bottles—the vermouth, the gin and all that."

"Where did you put them?"

"On the table there, sir."

She indicated a table by the wall.

"The tray with the glasses stood here, sir. Sir Charles, when he had finished mixing and shaking, poured out the cocktails into the glasses. Then I took the tray round and handed it to the ladies and gentlemen."

"Were all the cocktails on the tray you handed?"

"Sir Charles gave one to Miss Lytton Gore, sir—he was talking to her at the time—and he took his own. And Mr. Satterthwaite"—her eyes shifted to him for a moment—"came and fetched one for a lady—Miss Wills, I think it was."

"Quite right," said Mr. Satterthwaite.

"The others I handed, sir. I think everyone took one except Sir Bartholomew."

"Will you be so very obliging, Temple, as to repeat the performance? Let us put cushions for some of the people. I stood here, I remember; Miss Sutcliffe was there."

With Mr. Satterthwaite's help, the scene was reconstructed. Mr. Satterthwaite was observant. He remembered fairly well where everyone had been in the room. Then Temple did her round. They ascertained that she had started with Mrs. Dacres, gone on to Miss Sutcliffe and Poirot, and had then come to Mr. Babbington, Lady Mary and Mr. Satterthwaite, who had been sitting together.

This agreed with Mr. Satterthwaite's recollection.

Finally Temple was dismissed.

"Pah!" cried Poirot. "It does not make sense. Temple is the last person to handle those cocktails, but it was impossible for her to tamper with them in any way and, as I say, one cannot force a cocktail on a particular person."

"It's instinctive to take the one nearest to you," said Sir Charles.

"Possibly that might work by handing the tray to the person first, but even then it would be very uncertain. The glasses are close together; one does not look particularly nearer than another. No, no, such a haphazard method could not be adopted. Tell me, Mr. Satterthwaite, did Mr. Babbington put his cocktail down or did he retain it in his hand?"

"He put it down on this table."

"Did anyone come near that table after he had done so?"

"No. I was the nearest person to him and I assure you I did not tamper with it in any way, even if I could have done so unobserved."

Mr. Satterthwaite spoke rather stiffly. Poirot hastened to apologize:

"No, no, I am not making an accusation—*quelle idée!* But I want to be very sure of my facts. According to the analysis, there was nothing out of the way in that cocktail. Now, it seems that, apart from that analysis, there could have been nothing put in it. The same results from two different tests. But Mr. Babbington ate or drank nothing else, and if he was poisoned by pure nicotine, death would have resulted very rapidly. You see where that leads us?"

"Nowhere, damn it all," said Sir Charles.

"I would not say that—no, I would not say that. It suggests a very monstrous idea—which I hope and trust cannot be true. No, of course it is not true—the death of Sir Bartholomew proves that—and yet——"

He frowned, lost in thought. The others watched him curiously. He looked up.

"You see my point, do you not? Mrs. Babbington was not at Melfort Abbey; therefore Mrs. Babbington is cleared of suspicion."

"Mrs. Babbington—but no one has even dreamed of suspecting her."

Poirot smiled beneficently.

"No? It is curious, that. The idea occurred to me at once—but at once. If the poor gentleman is not poisoned by the cocktail, then he must have been poisoned a very few minutes before entering the house. What way could there be? A capsule? Something, perhaps, to prevent indigestion. But who, then, could tamper with that? Only a wife. Who might, perhaps, have a motive that no one outside could possibly suspect? Again a wife."

"But they were devoted to each other!" cried Egg indignantly. "You don't understand a bit!"

Poirot smiled kindly at her.

"No. That is valuable. You know, but I do not. I see the facts unbiased by any preconceived notions. And let me tell you something, mademoiselle. In the course of my experience I have known five cases of wives murdered by devoted husbands, and twenty-two of husbands murdered by devoted wives. *Les femmes,* they obviously keep up appearances better."

"I think you're perfectly horrid," said Egg. "I know the Babbingtons are not like that. It's—it's monstrous!"

"Murder is monstrous, mademoiselle," said Poirot, and there was a sudden sternness in his voice.

He went on in a lighter tone:

"But I, who see only the facts, agree that Mrs. Babbington did not do this thing. You see, she was not at Melfort Abbey. No, as Sir Charles has already said, the guilt must lie on a person who was present at both occasions—one of the seven on your list."

There was a silence.

"And how do you advise us to act?" asked Mr. Satterthwaite.

"You have doubtless already your plan," suggested Poirot.

Sir Charles cleared his throat.

"The only feasible thing seems to be a process of elimination," he said. "My idea was to take each person on that list and consider them guilty until they are proved innocent. I mean that we are able to feel convinced ourselves that there is a connection between that person and Stephen Babbington, and we are to use all our ingenuity to find out what that connection can be. If we find no connection, then we pass on to the next person."

"It is good psychology, that," approved Poirot. "And your methods?"

"That, we have not yet had time to discuss. We should welcome your advice on that point, M. Poirot. Perhaps you yourself——"

Poirot held up a hand.

"My friend, do not ask me to do anything of an active nature. It is my lifelong conviction that any problem is best solved by thought. Let me hold what is called, I believe, the watching brief. Continue your investigations which Sir Charles is so ably directing."

"And what about me?" thought Mr. Satterthwaite. "These actors! Always in the limelight, playing the star part!"

"You will, perhaps, from time to time, require what we may describe as counsel's opinion. Me, I am the counsel."

He smiled at Egg.

"Does that strike you as the sense, mademoiselle?"

"Excellent," said Egg. "I'm sure your experience will be very useful to us."

Her face looked relieved. She glanced at her watch and gave an exclamation.

"I must go home. Mother will have a fit."

"I'll drive you home," said Sir Charles.

They went out together.

CHAPTER XVII

"So, you see, the fish has risen," said Hercule Poirot.

Mr. Satterthwaite, who had been looking at the door which had just closed behind the other two, gave a start as he turned to Poirot. The latter was smiling with a hint of mockery.

"Yes, yes, do not deny it. Deliberately you showed me the bait that day in Monte Carlo. Is it not so? You showed me the paragraph in the paper. You hoped that it would arouse my interest—that I should occupy myself with the affair."

"It is true," confessed Mr. Satterthwaite. "But I thought that I had failed."

"No, no, you did not fail. You are a shrewd judge of human nature, my friend. I was suffering from ennui; I had—in the words of the child who was playing near us—'nothing to do.' You came at the psychological moment—and talking of that, how much crime depends, too, on that psychological moment. The crime, the psychology, they go hand in hand. But let us come back to our muttons. This is a crime very intriguing; it puzzles me completely."

"Which crime—the first or second?"

"There is only one; what you call the first and the second murder are only the two halves of the same crime. The second half is simple—the motive, the means adopted——"

Mr. Satterthwaite interrupted:

"Surely the means present an equal difficulty. There was no poison found in any of the wine and the food was eaten by everybody."

"No, no, it is quite different. In the first case it does not seem as though anybody could have poisoned Stephen Bab-

122

bington. Sir Charles, if he had wanted to, could have poisoned one of his guests, but not any particular guest. Temple might possibly have slipped something into the last glass on the tray, but Mr. Babbington's was not the last glass. No, the murder of Mr. Babbington seems so impossible that I still feel that perhaps it is impossible—that he died a natural death, after all. But that we shall soon know. The second case is different. Any one of the guests present, or the butler or parlormaid, could have poisoned Bartholomew Strange. That presents no difficulty whatever."

"I don't see——" began Mr. Satterthwaite.

Poirot swept on:

"I will prove that to you sometime by a little experiment. Let us pass on to another and most important matter. It is vital, you see—and you will see, I am sure; you have the sympathetic heart and the delicate understanding—that I must not play the part of what you call the spoilsport."

"You mean——" began Mr. Satterthwaite, with the beginning of a smile.

"That Sir Charles must have the star part! He is used to it. And, moreover, it is expected of him by someone else. Am I not right? It does not please mademoiselle at all that I come to concern myself in this matter."

"You are what we call 'quick on the uptake,' M. Poirot."

"Ah, that, it leaps to the eye! I am of a very susceptible nature; I wish to assist a love affair, not to hinder it. You and I, my friend, must work together in this—to the honor and glory of Charles Cartwright, is it not so? When the case is solved——"

"If——" said Mr. Satterthwaite mildly.

"When! I do not permit myself to fail."

"Never?" asked Mr. Satterthwaite searchingly.

"There have been times," said Poirot with dignity, "when, for a short time, I have been what I suppose you would call slow in the take up. I have not perceived the truth as soon as I might have done."

"But you've never failed altogether?"

The persistence of Mr. Satterthwaite was curiosity, pure and simple. He wondered.

"Eh bien," said Hercule Poirot. "Once. Long ago, in Belgium. We will not talk of it."

Mr. Satterthwaite, his curiosity—and his malice—satisfied, hastened to change the subject:

123

"Just so. You were saying that when the case is solved——"

"Sir Charles will have solved it. That is essential. I shall have been a little cog in the wheel." He spread out his hands. "Now and then, here and there, I shall say a little word—just one little word—a hint, no more. I desire no honor, no renown. I have all the renown I need."

Mr. Satterthwaite studied him with interest. He was amused by the naïve conceit, the immense egoism of the little man. But he did not make the easy mistake of considering it mere empty boasting. An Englishman is usually modest about what he does well, sometimes pleased with himself over something he does badly, but a Latin has a truer appreciation of his own powers. If he is clever he sees no reason for concealing the fact.

"I should like to know," said Mr. Satterthwaite—"it would interest me very much—just what do you yourself hope to get out of this business? Is it the excitement of the chase?"

Poirot shook his head.

"No, no, it is not that. Like the *chien de chasse,* I follow the scent, and I get excited; and once on the scent, I cannot be called off it. All that is true. But there is more. It is—how shall I put it?—a passion for getting at the truth. In all the world there is nothing so curious and so interesting and so beautiful as truth."

There was silence for a little while after Poirot's words.

Then he took up the paper on which Mr. Satterthwaite had carefully copied out the seven names, and read them aloud:

"Mrs. Dacres, Captain Dacres, Miss Wills, Miss Sutcliffe, Lady Mary Lytton Gore, Miss Lytton Gore, Oliver Manders.

"Yes," he said. "Suggestive, is it not?"

"What is suggestive about it?"

"The order in which the names occur."

"I don't think there is anything suggestive about it. We just wrote the names down without any particular order about it."

"Exactly. The list is headed by Mrs. Dacres. I deduce from that that she is considered the most likely person to have committed the crime."

"Not the most likely," said Mr. Satterthwaite. "The least unlikely would express it better."

"And a third phrase would express it better still. She is perhaps the person you would all prefer to have committed the crime."

Mr. Satterthwaite opened his lips impulsively, then met the gentle, quizzical gaze of Poirot's shining green eyes and altered what he had been about to say:

"I wonder—— Perhaps, M. Poirot, you are right. Unconsciously that may be true."

"I would like to ask you something, Mr. Satterthwaite."

"Certainly, certainly," Mr. Satterthwaite answered complacently.

"From what you have told me, I gather that Sir Charles and Miss Lytton Gore went together to interview Mrs. Babbington."

"Yes."

"You did not accompany them?"

"No. Three would have been rather a crowd."

Poirot smiled.

"And also, perhaps, your inclinations led you elsewhere. You had, as they say, different fish to fry. Where did you go, Mr. Satterthwaite?"

"I had tea with Lady Mary Lytton Gore," said Mr. Satterthwaite stiffly.

"And what did you talk about?"

"She was so good as to confide in me some of the troubles of her early married life."

He repeated the substance of Lady Mary's story. Poirot nodded his head sympathetically.

"That is so true to life—the idealistic young girl who marries the bad hat and will listen to nobody. But did you talk of nothing else? Did you, for instance, not speak of Mr. Oliver Manders?"

"As a matter of fact, we did."

"And you learned about him—what?"

Mr. Satterthwaite repeated what Lady Mary had told him. Then he said:

"What made you think we had talked of him?"

"Because you went there for that reason. . . . Oh, yes, do not protest. You may hope that Mrs. Dacres or her husband committed the crime, but you think that young Manders did."

He stilled Mr. Satterthwaite's protests:

"Yes, yes, you have the secretive nature. You have your ideas, but you like keeping them to yourself. I have sympathy with you. I do the same myself."

"I don't suspect him—that's absurd. But I just wanted to know more about him."

"That is as I say. He is your instinctive choice. I, too, am interested in that young man. I was interested in him on the night of the dinner here, because I saw——"

"What did you see?" asked Mr. Satterthwaite eagerly.

"I saw that there were two people at least—perhaps more—who were playing a part. One was Sir Charles." He smiled. "He was playing the naval officer; am I not right? That is quite natural. A great actor does not cease to act because he is not on the stage anymore. But young Manders, he, too, was acting. He was playing the part of the bored and blasé young man, but in reality he was neither bored nor blasé; he was very keenly alive. And therefore, my friend, I noticed him."

"How did you know I'd been wondering about him?"

"In many little ways. You had been interested in that accident of his that brought him to Melfort Abbey that night. You had not gone with Sir Charles and Miss Lytton Gore to see Mrs. Babbington. Why? Because you wanted to follow out some line of your own unobserved. You went to Lady Mary's to find out about someone. Who? It could only be someone local. Oliver Manders. And then—most characteristic—you put down his name at the bottom of the list. Who are really the most unlikely suspects in your mind—Lady Mary and Mademoiselle Egg?—but you put young Manders's name after theirs, because he is your dark horse and you want to keep him to yourself."

"Dear me," said Mr. Satterthwaite. "Am I really that kind of man?"

"*Précisément.* You have shrewd judgment and observation, and you like keeping its results to yourself. Your opinions of people are your private collection. You do not display them for all the world to see."

"I believe——" began Mr. Satterthwaite, but he was interrupted by the return of Sir Charles.

The actor came in with a springing, buoyant step.

"Br-r-r," he said. "It's a wild night."

He poured himself out a whisky and soda.

Mr. Satterthwaite and Poirot both declined.

126

"Well," said Sir Charles, "let's map out our plan of campaign.... Where's that list, Satterthwaite? ... Ah, thanks. ... Now, M. Poirot, counsel's opinion, if you please. How shall we divide up the spade work?"

"How would you suggest, yourself, Sir Charles?"

"Well, we might divide these people up—division of labor, eh? First, here's Mrs. Dacres. Egg seems rather keen to take her on. She seems to think that anyone so perfectly turned out won't get impartial treatment from mere males. It seems quite a good idea to approach her through the professional side. Satterthwaite and I might work the other gambit as well, if it seemed advisable. Then there's Dacres. I know some of his racing pals. I dare say I could pick up something that way. Then there's Angela Suttcliffe."

"That also seems to be your work, Cartwright," said Mr. Satterthwaite. "You know her pretty well, don't you?"

"Yes. That's why I'd rather somebody else tackled her. Firstly"—he smiled ruefully—"I shall be accused of not putting my back into the job and, secondly—well, she's a friend. You understand?"

"*Parfaitement, parfaitement.* You feel the natural delicacy. It is most understandable. This good Mr. Satterthwaite—he will replace you in the task."

"Lady Mary and Egg—they don't count, of course. What about young Manders? His presence on the night of Tollie's death was an accident; still, I suppose we ought to include him."

"Mr. Satterthwaite will look after young Manders," said Poirot. "But I think, Sir Charles, you have missed out a name on your list. You have passed over Miss Muriel Wills."

"So I have. Well, if Satterthwaite takes on Manders, I'll take on Miss Wills. Is that settled? Any suggestions, M. Poirot?"

"No, no, I do not think so. I shall be interested to hear your results."

"Of course; that goes without saying. Another idea. If we procured photographs of these people, we might use them in making inquiries in Gilling."

"Excellent," approved Poirot. "There was something—— Ah, yes, your friend, Sir Bartholomew, he did not drink cocktails, but he did drink the port?"

"Yes, he had a particular weakness for port."

"It seems odd to me that he did not taste anything unusual. Pure nicotine has a most pungent and unpleasant taste."

"You've got to remember," said Sir Charles, "that there probably wasn't any nicotine in the port. The contents of the glass were analyzed, remember."

"Ah, yes; foolish of me. But however it was administered, nicotine has a very disagreeable taste."

"I don't know that that would matter," said Sir Charles slowly. "Tollie had a very bad go of influenza last spring and it left him with his sense of taste and smell a good deal impaired."

"Ah, yes," said Poirot thoughtfully. "That might account for it. That simplifies things considerably."

Sir Charles went to the window and looked out.

"Still blowing a gale. I'll send for your things, M. Poirot. The Rose and Crown is all very well for enthusiastic artists, but I think you'd prefer proper sanitation and a comfortable bed."

"You are extremely amiable, Sir Charles."

"Not at all. I'll see to it now."

He left the room.

Poirot looked at Mr. Satterthwaite.

"If I may permit myself a suggestion."

"Yes?"

Poirot leaned forward and said in a low voice:

"Ask young Manders why he faked an accident. Tell him the police suspect him, and see what he says."

"You think——"

"I think nothing as yet, but there was the entry in the diary: 'Am worried about M.' It might conceivably stand for Manders. It might equally well be nothing whatever to do with the case."

"We shall see," said Mr. Satterthwaite.

"Yes, we shall see."

CHAPTER XVIII

THE showrooms of Ambrosine, Ltd., were very pure in appearance. The walls were a shade just off white; the thick pile carpet was so neutral as to be almost colorless; so was the upholstery. Chromium gleamed here and there, and on one wall was a gigantic geometric design in vivid blue and lemon yellow. The room had been designed by Mr. Sydney Sandford, the newest and youngest decorator of the moment.

Egg Lytton Gore sat in an armchair of modern design, faintly reminiscent of a dentist's chair, and watched exquisite snakelike young women with beautiful bored faces pass sinuously before her. Egg was principally concerned with endeavoring to appear as though fifty or sixty pounds was a mere bagatelle to pay for a dress.

Mrs. Dacres, looking, as usual, marvelously unreal, was—as Egg put it to herself—doing her stuff.

"Now, do you like this? Those shoulder knots—rather amusing, don't you think? And the waistline's rather penetrating. I shouldn't have the red-lead color, though; I should have it in the new color—Español—most attractive—like mustard with a dash of cayenne in it. How do you like Vin Ordinaire? Rather absurd, isn't it? Quite penetrating and ridiculous. Clothes simply must not be serious nowadays."

"It's very difficult to decide," said Egg. "You see"—she became confidential—"I've never been able to afford any clothes before. We were always so dreadfully poor. I remembered how simply marvelous you looked that night at Crow's Nest, and I thought, 'Now that I've got money to spend, I shall go to Mrs. Dacres and ask her to advise me.' I did admire you so much that night."

"My dear, how charming of you. I simply adore dressing a young girl. It's so important that girls shouldn't look raw, if you know what I mean."

"Nothing raw about you," thought Egg ungratefully. "Cooked to a turn, you are."

"You've got so much personality," continued Mrs. Dacres. "You mustn't have anything at all ordinary. Your clothes must be simple, and penetrating, and just faintly risible. You understand? Do you want several things?"

"I thought about four evening frocks, and a couple of day things, and a sports suit or two—that sort of thing."

The honey of Mrs. Dacres's manner became sweeter. It was fortunate that she did not know that at that moment Egg's bank balance was exactly fifteen pounds, twelve shillings, and that the said balance had got to last her until December.

More girls in gowns filed past Egg. In the intervals of technical conversation, Egg interspersed other matters.

"I suppose you've never been to Crow's Nest since," she said.

"No. My dear, I couldn't. It was so upsetting, and anyway, I always think Cornwall is rather terribly artisty. I simply cannot bear artists. Their bodies are always such a curious shape."

"It was a shattering business, wasn't it?" said Egg. "Old Mr. Babbington was rather a pet, too."

"Quite a period piece, I should imagine," said Mrs. Dacres. "You'd met him somewhere, hadn't you?"

"That dear old dugout? Had I? I don't remember."

"I think I remember his saying so," said Egg. "Not in Cornwall, though. I think it was at a place called Gilling."

"Was it?" Mrs. Dacres's eyes were vague. . . . "No, Marcelle, Petite Scandale is what I want—the Jenny model—and after that the blue Patou."

"Wasn't it extraordinary," said Egg, "about Sir Bartholomew being poisoned?"

"My dear, it was too penetrating for words! It's done me a world of good. All sorts of dreadful women come and order frocks from me just for the sensation. . . . Now, this Patou model would be perfect for you. Look at that perfectly useless and ridiculous frill; it makes the whole thing adorable. Young without being tiresome. . . . Yes, poor Sir Bartholomew's death has been rather a godsend to me. There's just an off chance, you see, that I might have murdered him. I've rather played up to that. Extraordinary fat women come and positively goggle at me. Too penetrating. And then, you see——"

But she was interrupted by the advent of a monumental American, evidently a valued client.

While the American was unburdening herself of her requirements, which sounded comprehensive and expensive, Egg managed to make an unobtrusive exit, telling the young lady who had succeeded Mrs. Dacres that she would think it over before making a final choice.

As she emerged into Bruton Street, Egg glanced at her watch. It was twenty minutes to one. Before very long she might be able to put her second plan into operation.

She walked as far as Berkeley Square and then slowly back again. At one o'clock she had her nose glued to a window displaying Chinese *objets d'art*.

Miss Doris Sims came rapidly out into Bruton Street and turned in the direction of Berkeley Square. Just before she got there, a voice spoke at her elbow.

"Excuse me," said Egg, "but can I speak to you a minute?"

The girl turned, surprised.

"You're one of the manikins at Ambrosine's, aren't you? I noticed you this morning. I hope you won't be frightfully offended if I say I think you've got simply the most perfect figure I've ever seen."

Doris Sims was not offended. She was merely slightly confused.

"It's very kind of you, I'm sure, madam," she said.

"You look frightfully good-natured too," said Egg. "That's why I'm going to ask you a favor. Will you have lunch with me at the Berkeley or the Ritz and let me tell you about it?"

After a moment's hesitation, Doris Sims agreed. She was curious and she liked good food.

Once established at a table and lunch ordered, Egg plunged into explanations.

"I hope you'll keep this to yourself," she said. "You see, I've got a job—writing up various professions for women. I want you to tell me all about the dressmaking business."

Doris looked slightly disappointed, but she complied ami-

131

ably enough, giving bald statements as to hours, rates of pay, conveniences and inconveniences of her employment. Egg entered particulars in a little notebook.

"It's awfully kind of you," she said. "I'm very stupid at this. It's quite new to me. You see, I'm frightfully bad off and this little bit of journalistic work will make all the difference."

She went on confidentially:

"It was rather nerve on my part walking into Ambrosine's and pretending I could buy lots of your models. Really, I've got just a few pounds of my dress allowance to last me till Christmas. I expect Mrs. Dacres would be simply wild if she knew."

Doris giggled.

"I should say she would."

"Did I do it well?" asked Egg. "Did I look as though I had money?"

"You did it splendidly, Miss Lytton Gore. Madam thinks you're going to get quite a lot of things."

"I'm afraid she'll be disappointed," said Egg.

Doris giggled more. She was enjoying her lunch and she felt attracted to Egg. "She may be a society young lady," she thought to herself, "but she doesn't put on airs. She's as natural as can be."

These pleasant relations once established, Egg found no difficulty in inducing her companion to talk freely on the subject of her employer.

"I always think," said Egg, "Mrs. Dacres looks a frightful cat. Is she?"

"None of us like her, Miss Lytton Gore, and that's a fact. But she's clever, of course, and she's got a rare head for business. Not like some society ladies who take up the dressmaking business and go bankrupt because their friends get clothes and don't pay. She's as hard as nails, madam is; though I will say she's fair enough, and she's got real taste; she knows what's what, and she's clever at getting people to have the style that suits them."

"I suppose she makes a lot of money."

A queer, knowing look came into Doris's eye.

"It's not for me to say anything, or to gossip."

"Of course not," said Egg. "Go on."

"But if you ask me, the firm's not far off Queer Street.

132

There was a Jewish gentleman came to see madam, and there have been one or two things—— It's my belief she's been borrowing to keep going, in the hope that trade would revive, and that she's got in deep. Really, Miss Lytton Gore, she looks terrible sometimes. Quite desperate. I don't know what she'd look like without her make-up. I don't believe she sleeps of nights."

"What's her husband like?"

"He's a queer fish. Bit of bad lot, if you ask me. Not that we ever see much of him. None of the other girls agree with me, but I believe she's very keen on him still. Of course, a lot of nasty things have been said."

"Such as?" asked Egg.

"Well, I don't like to repeat things. I never have been one for that."

"Of course not. Go on; you were saying——"

"Well, there's been a lot of talk among the girls. About a young fellow, very rich and very soft. Not exactly barmy, if you know what I mean—sort of betwixt and between. Madam's been running him for all she was worth. He might have put things right—he was soft enough for anything—but then he was ordered on a sea voyage, suddenly."

"Ordered by whom—a doctor?"

"Yes, someone in Harley Street. I believe now that it was the same doctor who was murdered up in Yorkshire—poisoned, so they said."

"Sir Bartholomew Strange?"

"That was the name. Madam was at the house party, and we girls said among ourselves—just laughing, you know—well, we said, supposing madam did him in—out of revenge, you know! Of course, it was just fun."

"Naturally," said Egg. "Girlish fun. I quite understand. You know, Mrs. Dacres is quite my idea of a murderess—so hard and remorseless."

"She's ever so hard—and she's got a wicked temper! When she lets go, there's not one of us dares to come near her. They say her husband's frightened of her—and no wonder."

"Have you ever heard her speak of anyone named Babbington or of a place called Gilling?"

"Really now, I can't call to mind that I have."

Doris looked at her watch and uttered an exclamation:

133

"Oh, dear, I must hurry. I shall be late."

"Good-bye and thanks so much for coming."

"It's been a pleasure, I'm sure. Good-bye, Miss Lytton Gore, and I hope the article will be a great success. I shall look out for it."

"You'll look in vain, my girl," thought Egg, as she asked for her bill.

Then, drawing a line through the supposed jottings for the article, she wrote in her little notebook:

> Cynthia Dacres. Believed to be in financial difficulties. Described as having a "wicked temper." Young man (rich) with whom she was believed to be having an affair was ordered on sea voyage by Sir Bartholomew Strange. Showed no reaction at mention of Gilling or at statement that Babbington knew her.

"There doesn't seem much there," said Egg to herself. "A possible motive for the murder of Sir Bartholomew, but very thin. M. Poirot may be able to make something of that. I can't."

CHAPTER XIX

BUT Egg had not yet finished her program for the day. Her next move was to the apartment house in which the Dacreses had a flat. The building was a new block of extremely expensive flats. There were sumptuous window boxes, and uniformed porters of such magnificence that they looked like foreign generals.

Egg did not enter the building. She strolled up and down on the opposite side of the street. After about an hour of this, she calculated that she must have walked several miles. It was half-past five.

Then a taxi drew up at the apartment house and Captain Dacres alighted from it. Egg allowed three minutes to elapse, then she crossed the road and entered the building.

Egg pressed the doorbell of No. 3. Dacres himself opened the door. He was still engaged in taking off his overcoat.

"Oh," said Egg. "How do you do. You do remember me, don't you? We met in Cornwall and again in Yorkshire."

"Of course—of course. In at the death both times, weren't we? Come in, Miss Lytton Gore."

"I wanted to see your wife. Is she in?"

"She's round in Bruton Street, at her dressmaking place."

"I know. I was there today. I thought perhaps she'd be back by now and that she wouldn't mind, perhaps, if I came here. Only, of course, I suppose I'm being a frightful bother."

Egg paused appealingly.

Freddie Dacres said to himself:

"Nice-looking filly. Damned pretty girl, in fact."

Aloud he said:

"Cynthia won't be back till well after six. I've just come

135

back from Newbury. Had a rotten day and left early. Come round to the club and have a cocktail."

Egg accepted, though she had a shrewd suspicion that Dacres had already had quite as much alcohol as was good for him.

Sitting in the underground dimness of the club, and sipping a martini, Egg said: "This is great fun. I've never been here before."

Freddie Dacres smiled indulgently. He liked a young and pretty girl. Not, perhaps, as much as he liked some other things, but well enough.

"Upsettin' sort of time, wasn't it?" he said. "Up in Yorkshire, I mean. Something rather amusin' about a doctor being poisoned—you see what I mean—wrong way about. A doctor's a chap who poisons other people."

He laughed uproariously at his own remark and ordered another pink gin.

"That's rather clever of you," said Egg. "I never thought of it that way before."

"Only a joke, of course," said Freddie Dacres.

"It's odd, isn't it," said Egg, "that when we meet, it's always at a death?"

"Bit odd," admitted Captain Dacres. "You mean the old clergyman chap at what's-his-name's—the actor fellow's place?"

"Yes. It was very queer, the way he died so suddenly."

"Damn disturbin'," said Dacres. "Makes you feel a bit gruey, fellows popping off all over the place. You know, you think, 'my turn next,' and it gives you the shivers."

"You knew Mr. Babbington before, didn't you? At Gilling."

"Don't know the place. No, I never set eyes on the old chap before. Funny thing is, he popped off just the same way as old Strange did. Bit odd, that. Can't have been bumped off, too, I suppose?"

"Well, what do you think?"

Dacres shook his head.

"Can't have been," he said decisively. "Nobody murders parsons. Doctors are different."

"Yes," said Egg, "I suppose doctors are different."

"Course they are. Stands to reason. Doctors are interfering devils." He slurred the words a little. He leaned forward. "Won't let well alone. Understand?"

"No," said Egg.

136

"They monkey about with fellows' lives. They've got too much power. Oughtn't to be allowed."

"I don't quite see what you mean."

"M'dear girl, I'm telling you. Get a fellow shut up—that's what I mean—put him in hell. They're cruel! Shut him up and keep the stuff from him, and however much you beg and pray, they won't give it you. Don't care a damn what torture you're in. That's doctors for you. I'm telling you—and I know."

His face twitched painfully. His little pin-point pupils stared past her.

"It's hell, I tell you—hell! And they call it curing you! Pretend they're doing a decent action. Swine!"

"Did Sir Bartholomew Strange——" began Egg cautiously.

He took the words out of her mouth.

"Sir Bartholomew Strange. Sir Bartholomew Humbug. I'd like to know what goes on in that precious sanatorium of his. Nerve cases. That's what they say. You're in there and you can't get out. And they say you've gone of your own free will. Free will. Just because they get hold of you when you've got the horrors."

He was shaking now. His mouth drooped suddenly.

"I'm all to pieces," he said apologetically. "All to pieces." He called to the waiter, pressed Egg to have another drink and, when she refused, ordered one himself.

"That's better," he said as he drained the glass.

"Got my nerve back now. Nasty business losing your nerve. Mustn't make Cynthia angry. She told me not to talk." He nodded his head once or twice. "Wouldn't do to tell the police all this," he said. "They might think I'd bumped old Strange off. Eh? You realize, don't you, that someone must have done it? One of us must have killed him. That's a funny thought. Which of us?—that's the question."

"Perhaps you know which," said Egg.

"What d'you say that for? Why should I know?"

He looked at her angrily and suspiciously.

"I don't know anything about it, I tell you. I wasn't going to take that damnable cure of his. No matter what Cynthia said, I wasn't going to take it. He was up to something—they were both up to something. But they couldn't fool me."

He drew himself up.

"I'm a shtrong man, Mish Lytton Gore."

"I'm sure you are," said Egg. "Tell me, do you know anything of a Mrs. de Rushbridger who is at the sanatorium?"

"Rushbridger? Rushbridger? Old Strange said something about her. Now, what was it? Can't remember. Can't remember anything."

He sighed, shook his head.

"Memory's going, that's what it is. And I've got enemies—a lot of enemies. They may be spying on me now."

He looked round uneasily. Then he leaned across the table to Egg.

"What was that woman doing in my room that day?"

"What woman?"

"Rabbit-faced woman. Writes plays. It was the morning after—after he died. I'd just come up from breakfast. She came out of my room and went through the baize door at the end of the passage—went through into the servants' quarters. Odd, eh? Why did she go into my room? What did she think she'd find there? What did she want to go nosing about for, anyway? What's it got to do with her?" He leaned forward confidentially. "Or do you think it's true, what Cynthia says?"

"What does Mrs. Dacres say?"

"Says I imagined it. Says I was 'seeing things.'" He laughed uncertainly. "I do see things now and again. Pink mice, snakes—all that sort of thing. But seein' a woman's different. I did see her. She's a queer fish, that woman. Nasty sort of eye she's got. Goes through you."

He leaned back on the soft couch. He seemed to be dropping asleep.

Egg got up.

"I must be going. Thank you very much, Captain Dacres.

"Don't thank me. Delighted. Absolutely delighted." His voice trailed off.

"I'd better go before he passes out altogether," thought Egg.

She emerged from the smoky atmosphere of the club into the cool evening air.

Beatrice, the housemaid, had said that Miss Wills poked and pried. Now came this story from Freddie Dacres. What had Miss Wills been looking for? What had she found? Was it possible that Miss Wills knew something?

Was there anything in this rather muddled story about Sir Bartholomew Strange? Had Freddie Dacres secretly feared and hated him?

It seemed possible.

But in all this no hint of any guilty knowledge in the Babbington case.

"How odd it would be," said Egg to herself, "if he wasn't murdered, after all."

And then she caught her breath sharply as she caught sight of the words on a newspaper placard a few feet away: CORNISH EXHUMATION CASE. RESULT.

Hastily, she held out a penny and snatched a paper. As she did so she collided with another woman doing the same thing. As Egg apologized she recognized Sir Charles's secretary, the efficient Miss Milray.

Standing side by side, they both sought the stop-press news. Yes, there it was.

RESULT OF CORNISH EXHUMATION. The words danced before Egg's eyes. Analysis of the organs. . . . Nicotine. . . .

"So he was murdered," said Egg.

"Oh, dear," said Miss Milray. "This is terrible—terrible."

Her rugged countenance was distorted with emotion. Egg looked at her in surprise. She had always regarded Miss Milray as something less than human.

"It upsets me," said Miss Milray, in explanation. "You see, I've known him all my life."

"Mr. Babbington?"

"Yes. You see, my mother lives at Gilling, where he used to be vicar. Naturally, it's upsetting."

"Oh, of course."

"The fact of the matter is," said Sir Charles's secretary, "I don't know what to do."

She flushed a little before Egg's look of astonishment.

"I'd like to write to Mrs. Babbington," she said quickly. "Only it doesn't seem quite—well, quite—— I don't know what I had better do about it."

Somehow, to Egg, the explanation was not quite satisfying.

CHAPTER XX

"Now, are you a friend, or are you a sleuth? I simply must know."

Miss Sutcliffe flashed a pair of mocking eyes as she spoke. She was sitting in a straight-backed chair, her gray hair becomingly arranged, her legs crossed, and Mr. Satterthwaite admired the perfection of her beautifully shod feet and her slender ankles. Miss Sutcliffe was a very fascinating woman, mainly owing to the fact that she seldom took anything seriously.

"Is that quite fair?" asked Mr. Satterthwaite.

"My dear man, of course it's fair. Have you come here for the sake of my beautiful eyes, as the French say so charmingly, or have you, you nasty man, come just to pump me about murders?"

"Can you doubt that your first alternative is the correct one?" asked Mr. Satterthwaite, with a little bow.

"I can and I do," said the actress with energy. "You are one of those people who look so mild and really wallow in blood."

"No, no."

"Yes, yes. The only thing I can't make up my mind about is whether it is an insult or a compliment to be considered a potential murderess. On the whole, I think it's a compliment."

She cocked her head a little on one side and smiled that slow, bewitching smile that never failed.

Mr. Satterthwaite thought to himself:

"Adorable creature."

Aloud he said: "I will admit, dear lady, that the death of

140

Sir Bartholomew Strange has interested me considerably. I have, as you perhaps know, dabbled in such things before."

He paused modestly, perhaps hoping that Miss Sutcliffe would show some knowledge of his activities. However, she merely asked:

"Tell me one thing. Is there anything in what that girl said?"

"Which girl and what did she say?"

"The Lytton Gore girl. The one who is so fascinated by Charles. . . . What a wretch Charles is; he will do it! . . . She thinks that that nice old man down in Cornwall was murdered too."

"What do you think?"

"Well, it certainly happened just the same way. She's an intelligent girl, you know. . . . Tell me; is Charles serious?"

"I expect your views on the subject are likely to be much more valuable than mine," said Mr. Satterthwaite.

"What a tiresomely discreet man you are!" cried Miss Sutcliffe. "Now, I"—she sighed—"am appallingly indiscreet."

She fluttered an eyelash at him.

"I know Charles pretty well. I know men pretty well. He seems to me to display all the signs of settling down. There's an air of virtue about him. He'll be handing round the plate and founding a family in record time—that's my view. How dull men are when they decide to settle down! They lose all their charm."

"I've often wondered why Sir Charles has never married," said Mr. Satterthwaite.

"My dear, he never showed any signs of wanting to marry. He wasn't what they call a marrying man. But he was a very attractive man." She sighed. A slight twinkle showed in her eyes as she looked at Mr. Satterthwaite. "He and I were once—well, why deny what everybody knows? It was very pleasant while it lasted, and we're still the best of friends. I suppose that's the reason the Lytton Gore child looks at me so fiercely. She suspects I still have a *tendresse* for Charles. Have I? Perhaps I have. But at any rate I haven't yet written my memoirs, describing all my affairs in detail, as most of my friends seem to have done. If I did, you know, the girl wouldn't like it. She'd be shocked. Modern girls are easily shocked. Her mother wouldn't be shocked at all. You can't really shock a sweet mid-Victorian. They say so little, but always think the worst."

Mr. Satterthwaite contented himself with saying:

"I think you are right in suspecting that Egg Lytton Gore mistrusts you."

Miss Sutcliffe frowned.

"I'm not at all sure that I'm not a little jealous of her. . . . We women are such cats, aren't we? Scratch, scratch, miauw, miauw, purr, purr."

She laughed.

"Why didn't Charles come and catechize me on this business? Too much nice feeling, I suppose. The man must think me guilty. . . . Am I guilty? What do you think now?"

She stood up and stretched out a hand.

> *"All the perfumes of Arabia will not sweeten this*
> *little hand."*

She broke off:

"No, I'm no Lady Macbeth. Comedy's my line."

"There seems also a certain lack of motive," said Mr. Satterthwaite.

"True. I liked Bartholomew Strange. We were friends. I had no reason for wishing him out of the way. Because we were friends, I'd rather like to take an active part in hunting down his murderer. Tell me if I can help in any way."

"I suppose, Miss Sutcliffe, you didn't see or hear anything that might have a bearing on the crime."

"Nothing that I haven't already told the police. The house party had only just arrived, you know. His death occurred on that first evening."

"The butler?"

"I hardly noticed him."

"Any peculiar behavior on the part of the guests?"

"No. Of course, that boy—what's his name?—Manders —turned up rather unexpectedly."

"Did Sir Bartholomew Strange seem surprised?"

"Yes, I think he was. He said to me, just before we went in to dinner, that it was an odd business—'a new method of gate crashing,' he called it. 'Only,' he said, 'it's my wall he's crashed, not my gate.'"

"Sir Bartholomew was in good spirits?"

"Very good spirits!"

"What about this secret passage you mentioned to the police?"

"I believe it led out of the library. Sir Bartholomew promised to show it to me, but of course the poor man died."

"How did the subject come up?"

"We were discussing a recent purchase of his—an old walnut bureau. I asked if it had a secret drawer in it. I told him I adored secret drawers. It's a passion of mine. And he said, no, there wasn't a secret drawer that he knew of, but he had got a secret passage in the house."

"Sir Bartholomew didn't mention a patient of his—a Mrs. de Rushbridger?"

"No."

"Do you know a place called Gilling?"

"Gilling? Gilling? No, I don't think I do. Why?"

"Well, you knew Mr. Babbington before, didn't you?"

"Who is Mr. Babbington?"

"The man who died, or who was killed, at Crow's Nest."

"Oh, the clergyman. I'd forgotten his name. No, I'd never seen him before in my life. Who told you I knew him?"

"Someone who ought to know," said Mr. Satterthwaite boldly.

Miss Sutcliffe seemed amused.

"Dear old man, did they think I'd had an affair with him? I must clear the poor man's memory. I'd never seen him before in my life."

And with that statement Mr. Satterthwaite was forced to rest content.

CHAPTER XXI

FIVE Upper Cathcart Road, Tooting, seemed an incongruous home for a satiric playwright. The room into which Sir Charles was shown had walls of a rather drab oatmeal color with a frieze of laburnum round the top. The curtains were of rose-colored velvet; there were a lot of photographs and china dogs; the telephone was coyly hidden by a lady with ruffled skirts; there were a great many little tables and some suspicious-looking brasswork from Birmingham via the Far East.

Miss Wills entered the room so noiselessly that Sir Charles, who was at the moment examining a ridiculously elongated Pierrot doll lying across the sofa, did not hear her. Her thin voice, saying, "How d'you do, Sir Charles. This is really a great pleasure," made him spin round.

Miss Wills was dressed in a limp jumper suit which hung disconsolately on her angular form. Her stockings were slightly wrinkled and she had on very high-heeled, patent-leather slippers.

Sir Charles shook hands, accepted a cigarette, and sat down on the sofa by the Pierrot doll. Miss Wills sat opposite him. The light from the window caught her pince-nez and made them give off little flashes.

"Fancy you finding me out here," said Miss Wills. "My mother will be ever so excited. She just adores the theater—especially anything romantic. That play where you were a prince at a university—she's often talked of it. She goes to matinées, you know, and eats chocolates—she's one of that kind. And she does love it."

144

"How delightful," said Sir Charles. "You don't know how charming it is to be remembered. The public memory is short."

He sighed.

"She'll be thrilled at meeting you," said Miss Wills. "Miss Sutcliffe came the other day and mother was thrilled at meeting her."

"Angela was here?"

"Yes. She's putting on a play of mine, you know. *Little Dog Laughed.*"

"Of course," said Sir Charles. "I've read about it. Rather intriguing title."

"I'm so glad you think so. Miss Sutcliffe likes it too. It's a kind of modern version of the nursery rhyme—a lot of froth and nonsense—hey-diddle-diddle and the dish-and-the-spoon scandal. Of course, it all revolves round Miss Sutcliffe's part—everyone dances to her fiddling—that's the idea."

Sir Charles said:

"Not bad. The world nowadays is rather like a mad nursery rhyme. 'The little dog laughed to see such sport,' eh?" And he thought suddenly: "Of course, this woman's the little dog. She looks on and laughs."

The light shifted from Miss Wills's pince-nez and he saw her pale-blue eyes regarding him intelligently through them.

"This woman," thought Sir Charles, "has a fiendish sense of humor."

Aloud he said:

"I wonder if you can guess what errand has brought me here."

"Well," said Miss Wills archly, "I don't suppose it was only to see poor little me."

Sir Charles registered for a moment the difference between the spoken and the written word. On paper Miss Wills was witty and cynical, in speech she was arch.

"It was really Satterthwaite put the idea into my head," said Sir Charles. "He fancies himself as being a good judge of character."

"He's very clever about people," said Miss Wills. "It's rather his hobby, I should say."

"And he is strongly of the opinion that if there were anything worth noticing that night at Melfort Abbey, you would have noticed it."

"Is that what he said?"

"Yes."

"I was very interested, I must admit," said Miss Wills slowly. "You see, I'd never seen a murder at close hand before. A writer's got to take everything as copy, hasn't she?"

"I believe that's a well-known axiom."

"So, naturally," said Miss Wills, "I tried to notice everything I could."

This was obviously Miss Wills's version of Beatrice's "poking and prying."

"About the guests?"

"About the guests."

"And what, exactly, did you notice?"

The pince-nez shifted.

"I didn't really find out anything; if I had, I'd have told the police, of course," she added virtuously.

"But you noticed things."

"I always do notice things. I can't help it. I'm funny that way." She giggled.

"And you noticed—what?"

"Oh, nothing—that is, nothing that you'd call anything. Just little odds and ends about people's characters. I find people so very interesting. So typical, if you know what I mean."

"Typical of what?"

"Of themselves. Oh, I can't explain. I'm ever so silly at saying things."

She giggled again.

"Your pen is deadlier than your tongue," said Sir Charles, smiling.

"I don't think it's very nice of you to say deadlier, Sir Charles."

"My dear Miss Wills, admit that with a pen in your hand you're quite merciless."

"I think you're horrid, Sir Charles. It's you who are merciless to me."

"I must get out of this bog of badinage," said Sir Charles to himself. He said aloud:

"So you didn't find out anything concrete, Miss Wills?"

"No, not exactly. At least, there was one thing. Something I noticed and ought to have told the police about, only I forgot."

"What was that?"

"The butler. He had a kind of strawberry mark on his left wrist. I noticed it when he was handing me vegetables. I suppose that's the sort of thing might come in useful."

"I should say very useful indeed. The police are trying hard to track down that man Ellis. Really, Miss Wills, you are a very remarkable woman. Not one of the servants or guests mentioned such a mark."

"Most people don't use their eyes much, do they?" said Miss Wills.

"Where, exactly, was the mark? And what size was it?"

"If you'll just stretch out your own wrist——" Sir Charles extended his arm. "Thank you. It was here." Miss Wills placed an unerring finger on the spot. "It was about the size, roughly, of a sixpence, and rather the shape of Australia."

"Thank you; that's very clear," said Sir Charles, removing his hands and pulling down his cuffs again.

"You think I ought to write to the police and tell them?"

"Certainly I do. It might be most valuable in tracing the man. Dash it all," went on Sir Charles, with feeling, "in detective stories there's always some identifying mark on the villain. I thought it was a bit hard that real life should prove so lamentably behindhand."

"It's usually a scar in stories," said Miss Wills thoughtfully.

"A birthmark's just as good," said Sir Charles.

He looked boyishly pleased.

"The trouble is," he went on, "most people are so indeterminate. There's nothing about them to take hold of."

Miss Wills looked inquiringly at him.

"Old Babbington, for instance," went on Sir Charles; "he had a curiously vague personality. Very difficult to lay hold of."

"His hands were very characteristic," said Miss Wills. "What I call a scholar's hands. A little crippled with arthritis, but very refined fingers and beautiful nails."

"What an observer you are. Ah, but—of course, you knew him before."

"Knew Mr. Babbington?"

"Yes, I remember his telling me so. Where was it he said he had known you?"

Miss Wills shook her head decisively.

"Not me. You must have been mixing me up with someone else—or he was. I'd never met him before."

"It must be my mistake. I thought—at Gilling——"

He looked at her keenly. Miss Wills appeared quite composed.

"No," she said.

"Did it ever occur to you, Miss Wills, that he might have been murdered too?"

"I know you and Miss Lytton Gore think so—or, rather, you think so."

"Oh—and—er—just what do you think?"

"It doesn't seem likely," said Miss Wills.

A little baffled by Miss Wills's clear lack of interest in the subject, Sir Charles started on another tack.

"Did Sir Bartholomew mention a Mrs. de Rushbridger at all?"

"No, I don't think so."

"She was a patient in his home. Suffering from nervous breakdown and loss of memory."

"He mentioned a case of lost memory," said Miss Wills. "He said you could hypnotize a person and bring their memory back."

"Did he, now? I wonder—— Could that be significant?"

Sir Charles frowned and remained lost in thought. Miss Wills said nothing.

"There's nothing else you could tell me? Nothing about any of the guests?"

It seemed to him that there was just the slightest pause before Miss Wills answered.

"No."

"About Mrs. Dacres? Or Captain Dacres? Or Miss Sutcliffe? Or Mr. Manders?"

He watched her very intently as he pronounced each name.

Once he thought he saw the pince-nez flicker, but he could not be sure.

"I'm afraid there's nothing I can tell you, Sir Charles."

"Oh, well!" He stood up. "Satterthwaite will be disappointed."

"I'm so sorry," said Miss Wills primly.

"I'm sorry, too, for disturbing you. I expect you were busy writing."

"I was, as a matter of fact."

"Another play?"

"Yes. To tell you the truth, I thought of using some of the characters at the house party at Melfort Abbey."

"What about libel?"

"That's quite all right, Sir Charles. I find people never recognize themselves." She giggled. "Not if, as you said just now, one is really merciless."

"You mean," said Sir Charles, "that we all have an exaggerated idea of our own personalities and don't recognize the truth if it's sufficiently brutally portrayed? I was quite right, Miss Wills; you are a cruel woman."

Miss Wills tittered.

"You needn't be afraid, Sir Charles. Women aren't usually cruel to men—unless it's some particular man; they're only cruel to other women."

"Meaning you've got your analytical knife into some unfortunate female. Which one? Well, perhaps I can guess. Cynthia's not beloved by her own sex."

Miss Wills said nothing. She continued to smile, rather a catlike smile.

"Do you write your stuff or dictate it?"

"Oh, I write it and send it to be typed."

"You ought to have a secretary."

"Perhaps. Have you still got that clever Miss—Miss Milray, wasn't it?"

"Yes, I've got Miss Milray. She went away for a time to look after her mother in the country, but she's back again now. Most efficient woman."

"So I should think. Perhaps a little impulsive."

"Impulsive? Miss Milray?"

Sir Charles stared. Never in his wildest flights of fancy had he associated impulse with Miss Milray.

"Only on occasions, perhaps," said Miss Wills.

Sir Charles shook his head.

"Miss Milray's the perfect robot. Good-bye, Miss Wills. Forgive me for bothering you, and don't forget to let the police know about that thingummybob."

"The mark on the butler's right wrist? No, I won't forget."

"Well, good-bye. . . . Half a sec. Did you say 'right wrist'? You said left just now."

"Did I? How stupid of me."

"Well, which was it?"

Miss Wills frowned and half closed her eyes.

"Let me see. I was sitting so—and he—— Would you mind, Sir Charles, handing me that brass plate as thought it was a vegetable dish? Left side."

Sir Charles presented the beaten-brass atrocity as directed.

"Cabbage, madam?"

"Thank you," said Miss Wills. "I'm quite sure now. It was the left wrist, as I said first. Stupid of me."

"No, no," said Sir Charles. "Left and right are always puzzling."

He said good-bye for the third time.

As he closed the door, he looked back. Miss Wills was not looking at him. She was standing where he had left her. She was gazing at the fire and on her lips was a smile of satisfied malice.

Sir Charles was startled.

"That woman knows something," he said to himself. "I'll swear she knows something. And she won't say—— But what the devil is it she knows?"

Chapter XXII

AT the office of Messrs. Speier & Ross, Mr. Satterthwaite asked for Mr. Oliver Manders and sent in his card.

Presently he was ushered into a small room where Oliver was sitting at a writing table.

The young man got up and shook hands.

"Good of you to look me up, sir," he said.

His tone implied:

"I have to say that, but really it's a damned bore."

Mr. Satterthwaite, however, was not easily put off.

He sat down, blew his nose thoughtfully, and peering over the top of his handkerchief, said:

"Seen the news this morning?"

"You mean the new financial situation? Well, the dollar——"

"Not dollars," said Mr. Satterthwaite. "Death. The result of the Loomouth exhumation. Babbington was poisoned. By nicotine."

"Oh, that; yes, I saw that. Our energetic Egg will be pleased. She always insisted it was murder."

"But it doesn't interest you?"

"My tastes aren't so crude. After all, murder——" He shrugged his shoulders. "So violent and inartistic."

"Not always inartistic," said Mr. Satterthwaite.

"No? Well, perhaps not."

"It depends, does it not, on who commits the murder? You, for instance, would, I am sure, commit a murder in a very artistic manner."

"Nice of you to say so," drawled Oliver.

151

"But frankly, my dear boy, I don't think much of the accident you faked. No more do the police, I understand."

There was a moment's silence; then a pen dropped to the floor.

Oliver said:

"Excuse me, I don't quite understand you."

"That rather inartistic performance of yours at Melfort Abbey. I should be interested to know just why you did it."

There was another silence, then Oliver said:

"You say the police suspect?"

Mr. Satterthwaite nodded.

"It looks a little suspicious, don't you think?" he asked pleasantly. "But perhaps you have a perfectly good explanation."

"I've got an explanation," said Oliver slowly. "Whether it's a good one or not, I don't know."

"Will you let me judge?"

There was a pause, then Oliver said:

"I came there the way I did, at Sir Bartholomew's own suggestion."

"What?" Mr. Satterthwaite was astonished.

"A bit odd, isn't it? But it's true. I got a letter from him suggesting that I should have a sham accident and claim hospitality. He said he couldn't put his reasons in writing, but he would explain them to me at the first opportunity."

"And did he explain?"

"No, he didn't. I got there just before dinner. I didn't see him alone. At the end of dinner he—he died."

The weariness had gone out of Oliver's manner. His dark eyes were fixed on Mr. Satterthwaite. He seemed to be studying attentively the reactions aroused by his words.

"You've got this letter?"

"No, I tore it up."

"A pity," said Mr. Satterthwaite dryly. "And you said nothing to the police?"

"No, it all seemed—well, rather fantastic."

"It is fantastic."

Mr. Satterthwaite shook his head. Had Bartholomew Strange written such a letter? It seemed highly uncharacteristic. The story had a melodramatic touch most unlike the physician's cheerful common sense.

152

He looked up at the young man. Oliver was still watching him. Mr. Satterthwaite thought: "He's looking to see if I swallow this story."

He said: "And Sir Bartholomew gave absolutely no reason for his request?"

"None whatever."

"An extraordinary story."

Oliver did not speak.

"Yet you obeyed the summons?"

Something of the weary manner returned.

"Yes, it seemed refreshingly out of the way to a somewhat jaded palate. I was curious, I must confess."

"Is there anything else?" asked Mr. Satterthwaite.

"What do you mean, sir—anything else?"

Mr. Satterthwaite did not really know what he meant. He was led by some obscure instinct.

"I mean," he said, "is there anything else that might tell against you?"

There was a pause. Then the young man shrugged his shoulders.

"I suppose I might as well make a clean breast of it. The woman isn't likely to hold her tongue about it."

Mr. Satterthwaite looked a question.

"It was the morning after the murder stuff. I was talking to the Anthony Astor woman. I took out my pocketbook, and something fell out of it. She picked it up and handed it back to me."

"And this something?"

"Unfortunately, she glanced at it before returning it to me. It was a cutting from a newspaper about nicotine—what a deadly poison it was, and so on."

"How did you come to have such an interest in the subject?"

"I didn't. I suppose I must have put that cutting in my wallet sometime or other, but I can't remember doing so. Bit awkward, eh?"

Mr. Satterthwaite thought: "A thin story."

"I suppose," went on Oliver Manders, "she went to the police about it."

Mr. Satterthwaite shook his head.

"I don't think so. I fancy she's a woman who likes—well, to keep things to herself. She's a collector of knowledge."

Oliver Manders leaned forward suddenly.

"I'm innocent, sir—absolutely innocent."

"I haven't suggested that you are guilty," said Mr. Satterthwaite mildly.

"But someone has—someone must have done. Someone has put the police onto me."

Mr. Satterthwaite shook his head.

"No, no."

"Then why did you come here today?"

"Partly as the result of my—er—investigations on the spot." Mr. Satterthwaite spoke a little pompously. "And partly at the suggestion of a friend."

"What friend?"

"Hercule Poirot."

"That man!" The expression burst from Oliver. "Is he back in England?"

"Yes."

"Why has he come back?"

Mr. Satterthwaite rose.

"Why does a dog go hunting?" he inquired.

And rather pleased with his retort, he left the room.

CHAPTER XXIII

SITTING in a comfortable armchair in his slightly florid suite at the Ritz, Hercule Poirot listened.

Egg was perched on the arm of a chair, Sir Charles stood in front of the fireplace, Mr. Satterthwaite sat a little farther away, observing the group.

"It's a failure all along the line," said Egg.

Poirot shook his head gently.

"No, no, you exaggerate. As regards a link with Mr. Babbington, you have drawn the blank, yes; but you have collected other suggestive information."

"The Wills woman knows something," said Sir Charles. "I'll swear she knows something."

"And Captain Dacres, he, too, has not the clear conscience. And Mrs. Dacres was desperately in want of money, and Sir Bartholomew spoiled her chance of laying hold of some."

"What do you think of young Manders's story?" asked Mr. Satterthwaite.

"It strikes me as peculiar and as being highly uncharacteristic of the late Sir Bartholomew Strange."

"You mean it's a lie?" asked Sir Charles bluntly.

"There are so many kinds of lies," said Hercule Poirot.

He was silent for a minute or two; then he said:

"This Miss Wills—she has written a play for Miss Sutcliffe?"

"Yes. The first night is Wednesday next."

"Ah!"

He was silent again. Egg said:

155

"Tell us, what shall we do now?"

The little man smiled at her.

"There is only one thing to do—think."

"Think?" cried Egg. Her voice was disgusted.

Poirot beamed on her.

"But yes, exactly that. Think! With thought, all problems can be solved."

"Can't we do something?"

"For you the action, eh, mademoiselle? But certainly, there are still things you can do. There is, for instance, this place, Gilling, where Mr. Babbington lived for so many years. You can make inquiries there. You say that this Miss Milray's mother lives at Gilling and is an invalid. An invalid knows everything. She hears everything and forgets nothing. Make your inquiries of her. It may lead to something. Who knows?"

"Aren't you going to do anything?" demanded Egg persistently.

Poirot twinkled.

"You insist that I, too, shall be active? *Eh bien,* it shall be as you wish. Only me, I shall not leave this place. I am very comfortable here. But I will tell you what I will do. I will give the party—the sherry party. That is fashionable, is it not?"

"A sherry party?"

"Précisément, and to it I will ask Mrs. Dacres, Captain Dacres, Miss Sutcliffe, Miss Wills, Mr. Manders and your charming mother, mademoiselle."

"And me?"

"Naturally, and you. The present company is included."

"Hurrah," said Egg. "You can't deceive me, M. Poirot. Something will happen at that party. It will, won't it?"

"We shall see," said Poirot. "But do not expect too much, mademoiselle. Now leave me with Sir Charles, for there are a few things about which I want to ask his advice."

As Egg and Mr. Satterthwaite stood waiting for the lift, Egg said ecstatically:

"It's lovely—just like detective stories. All the people will be there and then he'll tell us which of them did it."

"I wonder," said Mr. Satterthwaite.

The sherry party took place on Monday evening. The invitation had been accepted by all.

The charming and indiscreet Miss Sutcliffe laughed mischievously as she glanced round.

"Quite the spider's parlor, M. Poirot. And here all we poor little flies have walked in. I'm sure you're going to give us the most marvelous résumé of the case, and then suddenly you'll point at me and say 'Thou art the woman,' and everyone will say 'She done it,' and I shall burst into tears and confess, because I'm too terribly suggestible for words. Oh, M. Poirot, I'm so frightened of you."

"Quelle histoire," cried Poirot. He was busy with a decanter and glasses. He handed her a glass of sherry with a bow. "This is a friendly little party. Do not let us talk of murders and bloodshed and poison. La, la! These things, they spoil the palate."

He handed a glass to the grim Miss Milray, who had accompanied Sir Charles and was standing with a forbidding expression on her face.

"Voilà," said Poirot as he finished dispensing hospitality. "Let us forget the grim occasion on which we first met. Let us have the party spirit. Eat, drink, and be merry, for tomorrow we die. Ah, malheur, I have again mentioned death. Madame"—he bowed to Mrs. Dacres—"may I be permitted to wish you good luck and congratulate you on your very charming gown?"

"Here's to you, Egg," said Sir Charles.

"Cheerio," said Freddie Dacres.

Everybody murmured something. There was an air of forced gaiety about the proceedings. Everyone was determined to appear gay and unconcerned. Only Poirot himself seemed naturally so. He rambled on happily:

"The sherry, I prefer it to the cocktail, and a thousand thousand times to the whisky. Ah, quelle horreur, the whisky. But drinking the whisky, you ruin—absolutely ruin—the palate. The delicate wines of France, to appreciate them, you must never, never—— Ah, qu'est-çe qu'il y a?"

A strange sound had interrupted him—a kind of choking cry. Every eye went to Sir Charles, as he stood swaying, his face convulsed. The glass dropped from his hand onto the carpet; he took a few steps blindly, then collapsed.

There was a moment's stupefied silence. Then Angela Sutcliffe screamed and Egg started forward.

"Charles!" cried Egg. "Charles!"

She fought her way blindly forward. Mr. Satterthwaite gently held her back.

"Oh, dear God!" cried Lady Mary. "Not another!"

Angela Sutcliffe cried out:

"He's been poisoned too! This is awful! Oh, my God, this is too awful!"

And suddenly collapsing onto a sofa, she began to sob and laugh—a horrible sound.

Poirot had taken charge of the situation. He was kneeling by the prostrate man. The others drew back while he made his examination. He rose to his feet, mechanically dusting the knees of his trousers. He looked round at the assembly. There was complete silence, except for the smothered sobs of Angela Sutcliffe.

"My friend——" began Hercule Poirot.

He got no further, for Egg spat out at him:

"You fool! You absurd play-acting little fool! Pretending to be so great and so wonderful and to know all about everything! And now you let this happen! Another murder! Under your very nose! If you'd let the whole thing alone, this wouldn't have happened! It's you who have murdered Charles—you—you—you——"

She stopped, unable to get out the words.

Poirot nodded his head gravely and sadly.

"It is true, mademoiselle. I confess it. It is I who have murdered Sir Charles. But I, mademoiselle, am a very special kind of murderer. I can kill—and I can restore to life." He turned and in a different tone of voice, an apologetic everyday voice, he said:

"A magnificent performance, Sir Charles. I congratulate you. Perhaps you would now like to take your curtain."

With a laugh the actor sprang to his feet and bowed mockingly.

Egg gave a great gasp.

"M. Poirot, you—you beast!"

"Charles!" cried Angela Sutcliffe. "You complete devil!"

"But why——"

"How——"

"What on earth——"

By means of his upraised hand, Poirot obtained silence.

"Messieurs, mesdames. I demand pardon of you all. This little farce was necessary to prove to you all, and, incidentally, to prove to myself, a fact which my reason already told me is true.

"Listen. On this tray of glasses I placed in one glass a teaspoonful of plain water. That water represented pure nicotine. These glasses are of the same kind as those possessed by Sir Charles Cartwright and by Sir Bartholomew Strange. Owing to the heavy cut glass, a small quantity of a colorless liquid is quite undetectable. Imagine then the port glass of Sir Batholomew Strange. After it was put on the table, somebody introduced into it a sufficient quantity of pure nicotine. That might have been done by anybody—the butler, the parlormaid or one of the guests who slipped into the dining room on his or her way downstairs. Dessert arrives, the port is taken round, the glass is filled. Sir Bartholomew drinks, and dies.

"Tonight we have played a third tragedy—a sham tragedy. I asked Sir Charles to play the part of the victim. This he did magnificently. Now suppose for a minute that this was not a farce, but truth. Sir Charles is dead. What will be the steps taken by the police?"

Miss Sutcliffe cried:

"Why, the glass, of course." She nodded to where the glass lay on the floor as it had fallen from Sir Charles's hand. "You only put water in, but if it had been nicotine——"

"Let us suppose it was nicotine." Poirot touched the glass gently with his toe. "You are of the opinion that the police would analyze the glass and that traces of nicotine would be found?"

"Certainly."

Poirot shook his head gently.

"You are wrong. No nicotine would be found."

They stared at him.

"You see"—he smiled—"that is not the glass from which Sir Charles drank." With an apologetic grin, he extracted a glass from the tail pocket of his coat. "This is the glass that he used."

He went on.

"It is, you see, the simple theory of the conjuring trick. The attention cannot be in two places at once. To do my conjuring trick I need the attention focused elsewhere. Well, there is a moment, a psychological moment. When Sir Charles falls dead, every eye in the room is on his dead body. Everyone crowds forward to get near him. And no one—no one at all—looks at Hercule Poirot. And in that moment I exchange the glasses and no one sees.

"So, you see, I prove my point. There was such a moment at Crow's Nest, there was such a moment at Melfort Abbey— and so, there was nothing in the cocktail glass and nothing in the port glass."

Egg cried:

"Who changed them?"

Looking at her, Poirot replied:

"That we have still to find out."

"You don't know?"

Poirot shrugged his shoulders.

Rather uncertainly, the guests made signs of departure. Their manner was a little cold. They felt they had been badly fooled.

With a gesture of the hand, Poirot arrested them.

"One little moment, I pray of you. There is one thing more that I have to say. Tonight, admittedly, we have played the comedy. But that comedy may be played in earnest; it may become a tragedy. Under certain conditions, the murderer may strike a third time. I speak now to all of you here present. If any one of you knows something—something that may bear in any way on this crime, I implore that person to speak now. To keep knowledge to oneself at this juncture may be dangerous—so dangerous that death may be the result of silence. Therefore, I beg again, if anyone knows anything, let that person speak now before it is too late."

It seemed to Sir Charles that Poirot's appeal was addressed especially to Miss Wills. If so, it had no result. Nobody spoke or answered.

Poirot sighed. His hand fell.

"Be it so, then. I have given warning. I can do no more. Remember, to keep silence is dangerous."

But still nobody spoke.

Awkwardly, the guests departed.

Egg, Sir Charles and Mr. Satterthwaite were left.

Egg had not yet forgiven Poirot. She sat very still, her

cheeks flushed and her eyes angry. She wouldn't look at Sir Charles.

"That was a clever bit of work, Poirot," said Sir Charles appreciatively.

"Amazing," said Mr. Satterthwaite with a chuckle. "I wouldn't have believed that I wouldn't have seen you do that exchange."

"That is why," said Poirot, "I could take no one into my confidence. The experiment could only be fair this way."

"Was that the only reason you planned this—to see whether it could be done unnoticed?"

"Well, not quite, perhaps. I had one other aim."

"Yes?"

"I wanted to watch the expression on one person's face when Sir Charles fell dead."

"Which person's?" said Egg sharply.

"Ah, that is my secret."

"And you did watch that person's face?" said Mr. Satterthwaite.

"Yes."

"Well?"

Poirot did not reply. He merely shook his head.

"Won't you tell us what you saw there?"

Poirot said slowly:

"I saw an expression of the utmost surprise."

Egg drew her breath in sharply.

"You mean," she said, "that you know who the murderer is?"

"You can put it that way if you like, mademoiselle."

"But then—but then, you know everything."

Poirot shook his head.

"No, on the contrary, I know nothing at all. For, you see, I do not know why Stephen Babbington was killed. Until I know that, I can prove nothing. I can know nothing. It all hinges on that—the motive for Stephen Babbington's death."

There was a knock at the door and a page entered with a telegram on a tray.

Poirot opened it. His face changed. He handed the telegram to Sir Charles. Leaning over Sir Charles's shoulder, Egg read it aloud:

PLEASE COME AND SEE ME AT ONCE STOP CAN GIVE YOU
VALUABLE INFORMATION AS TO BARTHOLOMEW STRANGE'S
DEATH

MARGARET DE RUSHBRIDGER

"Mrs. de Rushbridger!" cried Sir Charles. "We were
right, after all! She has got something to do with the case."
And he added: "Margaret—M. The initial in Tollie's diary.
At last we're getting somewhere."

CHAPTER XXIV

AT once an excited discussion sprang up. An A.B.C. was produced. It was decided that an early train would be better than going by car.

"At last," said Sir Charles, "we're going to get that particular part of the mystery cleared up."

"What do you think the mystery is?" asked Egg.

"I can't imagine. But it can't fail to throw some light on the Babbington affair. If Tollie got those people together on purpose, as I feel pretty sure he did, then the 'surprise' he talked of springing on them had something to do with this Rushbridger woman. I think we can assume that, don't you, M. Poirot?"

Poirot shook his head in a perplexed manner.

"This telegram complicates the affair," he murmured. "But we must be quick—extremely quick."

Mr. Satterthwaite did not see the need for extreme haste, but he agreed politely.

"Certainly, we will go by the first train in the morning. Er—that is to say, is it necessary for us all to go?"

"Sir Charles and I had arranged to go down to Gilling," said Egg.

"We can postpone that," said Sir Charles.

"I don't think we ought to postpone anything," said Egg. "There is no need for all four of us to go to Yorkshire. It's absurd. Mass formation. M. Poirot and Mr. Satterthwaite go to Yorkshire and Sir Charles and I go to Gilling."

"I'd rather like to look into this Rushbridger business," said Sir Charles, with a trace of wistfulness. "You see, I—er—talked to the matron before—got my foot in, so to speak."

163

"That's just why you'd better keep away," said Egg. "You involved yourself in a lot of lies, and now that this Rushbridger woman has come to herself, you'll be exposed as a thorough-paced liar. It's far, far more important that you should come to Gilling. If we want to see Miss Milray's mother, she'll open out to you far more than she would to anyone else. You're her daughter's employer and she'll have confidence in you."

Sir Charles looked into Egg's glowing earnest face.

"I'll come to Gilling," he said. "I think you're quite right."

"I know I'm right," said Egg.

"In my opinion, an excellent arrangement," said Poirot briskly. "As mademoiselle says, Sir Charles is preeminently the person to interview this Mrs. Milray. Who knows, you may learn from her facts of much more importance than we shall learn in Yorkshire."

Matters were arranged on this basis, and the following morning Sir Charles picked up Egg in his car at a quarter to ten. Poirot and Mr. Satterthwaite had already left London by train.

It was a lovely crisp morning, with just a touch of frost in the air. Egg felt her spirits rising as they turned and twisted through the various shortcuts which Sir Charles's experience had discovered south of the Thames.

At last, however, they were flying smoothly along the Folkestone road. After passing through Maidstone, Sir Charles consulted a map and they turned off from the main road and were shortly winding through country lanes. It was about a quarter to twelve when they at last reached their objective.

Gilling was a village which the world had left behind. It had an old church, a vicarage, two or three shops, a row of cottages, three or four new council houses and a very attractive village green.

Miss Milray's mother lived in a tiny house on the other side of the green from the church.

As the car drew up, Egg asked:

"Does Miss Milray know you are going to see her mother?"

"Oh, yes. She wrote to prepare the old lady."

"Do you think that was a good thing?"

"My dear child, why not?"

"Oh, I don't know. You didn't bring her down with you, though."

164

"As a matter of fact, I thought she might cramp my style. She's so much more efficient than I am; she'd probably try to prompt me."

Egg laughed.

Mrs. Milray turned out to be almost ludicrously unlike her daughter. Where Miss Milray was hard, she was soft; where Miss Milray was angular, she was round. Mrs. Milray was an immense dumpling of a woman, immovably fixed in an armchair conveniently placed, so that she would, from the window, observe all that went on in the world outside.

She seemed pleasurably excited by the arrival of her visitors.

"This is very nice of you, I'm sure, Sir Charles. I've heard so much about you from my Violet." Violet—singularly incongruous name for Miss Milray. "You don't know how much she admires you. It's been most interesting for her, working with you all these years.... Won't you sit down, Miss Lytton Gore? You'll excuse my not getting up. I've lost the use of my limbs for many years now. The Lord's will, and I don't complain, and what I say is, one can get used to anything. Perhaps you'd like a little refreshment after your drive down?"

Both Sir Charles and Egg disclaimed the need of refreshment, but Mrs. Milray paid no attention. She clapped her hands in an Oriental manner, and tea and biscuits made their appearance. As they nibbled and sipped, Sir Charles came to the object of their visit.

"I expect you've heard, Mrs. Milray, all about the tragic death of Mr. Babbington, who used to be vicar here?"

The dumpling nodded its head in vigorous assent.

"Yes, indeed. I've read all about the exhumation in the paper. And whoever can have poisoned him I can't imagine. A very nice man, he was; everyone liked him here—and her too. And their little children and all."

"It is indeed a great mystery," said Sir Charles. "We're all in despair about it. In fact, we wondered if you could possibly throw any light upon the matter."

"Me? But I haven't seen the Babbingtons—— Let me see. It must be over fifteen years."

"I know, but some of us have the idea that there might be something in the past to account for his death."

"I'm sure I don't know what there could be. They led very quiet lives. Very badly off, poor things, with all those children."

Mrs. Milray was willing enough to reminisce, but her reminiscences seemed to shed little light on the problem they had set out to solve.

Sir Charles showed her the enlargement of a snapshot which included the Dacres, also an early portrait of Angela Sutcliffe and a somewhat blurred reproduction of Miss Wills, cut from a newspaper.

Mrs. Milray surveyed them all with great interest, but with no signs of recognition.

"I can't say I remember any of them. Of course, it's a long time ago. But this is a small place. There's not much coming and going. The Agnew girls—the doctor's daughters—they're all married and out in the world; and our present doctor's a bachelor; he's got a new young partner. Then there were the old Miss Cayleys—sat in the big pew—they're all dead many years back. And the Richardsons—he died and she went to Wales—and the village people, of course. But there's not much change there. Violet, I expect, could tell you as much as I could. She was a young girl then, and often over at the vicarage."

Sir Charles tried to envisage Miss Violet Milray as a young girl, and failed.

He asked Mrs. Milray if she remembered anyone of the name of Rushbridger, but the name failed to evoke any response.

Finally they took their leave.

Their next move was a scratch lunch in the baker's shop. Sir Charles had hankerings for fleshpots elsewhere, but Egg pointed out that they might get hold of some local gossip.

"And boiled eggs and scones will do you no harm for once," she said severely. "Men are so fussy about their food."

"I always find eggs so depressing," said Sir Charles meekly.

The woman who served them was communicative enough. She, too, had read of the exhumation in the paper and had been proportionately thrilled by its being "old vicar." "I was a child at the time," she explained, "but I remember him."

She could not, however, tell them much about him.

After lunch they went to the church and looked through

the register of births, marriages and deaths. Here again, there seemed nothing hopeful or suggestive.

They came out into the churchyard and lingered. Egg read the names on the tombstones.

"What queer names there are," she said. "Listen, here's a whole family of Stavepennys, and here's a Mary Ann Stickle-path."

"None of them so queer as mine," murmured Sir Charles.

"Cartwright? I don't think that's a queer name at all."

"I didn't mean Cartwright. Cartwright's my acting name and I finally adopted it legally."

"What's your real name?"

"I couldn't possibly tell you. It's my guilty secret."

"Is it as terrible as all that?"

"It's not so much terrible as humorous."

"Oh, tell it to me."

"Certainly not," said Sir Charles firmly.

"Please."

"No."

"Why not?"

"You'd laugh."

"I wouldn't."

"You wouldn't be able to help laughing."

"Oh, please tell me. Please, please, please."

"What a persistent creature you are, Egg. Why do you want to know?"

"Because you won't tell me."

"You adorable child," said Sir Charles.

"I'm not a child."

"Aren't you? I wonder."

"Tell me," whispered Egg softly.

A humorous and rueful smile twisted Sir Charles's mouth.

"Very well, here goes. My father's name was Mugg."

"Not really?"

"Really and truly."

"H'm," said Egg. "That is a bit catastrophic. To go through life as Mugg."

"Wouldn't have taken me far in my career, I agree. I remember," went on Sir Charles dreamily, "I played with the idea—I was young then—of calling myself Ludovic Castiglione, but I eventually compromised on British alliteration as Charles Cartwright."

"Are you really Charles?"

"Yes, my godfathers and godmothers saw to that." He hesitated, then said: "Why don't you say Charles, and drop the Sir?"

"I might."

"You did yesterday. When—when you thought I was dead."

"Oh, then."

Egg tried to make her voice sound nonchalant. For some reason or other, she felt it was imperative to change the subject. She hurried on:

"I wonder what Oliver is doing today?"

"Manders? Why do you want to think about him?"

Egg said: "I'm very fond of Oliver."

Somehow, it pleased her to say that. She stole a glance sideways at Sir Charles. Would he look at all jealous? Certainly he was frowning.

Then suddenly Egg felt a twinge of remorse. Poor Oliver. It was a shame dragging him in like that.

She said: "It's getting cold; let's go."

She shivered as she spoke. The sun had gone in.

She thought: "What a funny feeling I've got. It might be a premonition."

She shivered again.

"I wonder," she said, "if the others have found out anything?"

Sir Charles seemed absent-minded.

"The others? What others?"

"In Yorkshire."

"Somehow," said Sir Charles, "today I don't feel as though I cared."

"Charles, you used to be so keen."

But Sir Charles was no longer playing the part of the great detective.

"Well, it was my own show. Now I've handed it over to Mustachios. It's his business."

"Do you think he really knows who committed the crimes? He said he did."

"Probably hasn't the faintest idea, but he's got to keep up his professional reputation."

Egg was silent. Sir Charles said:

"What are you thinking about?"

"I was thinking about Miss Milray. She was so odd in her manner that evening I told you about. She had just bought the paper about the exhumation and she said she didn't know what to do."

"Nonsense," said Sir Charles cheerfully. "That woman always knows what to do."

"Do be serious, Charles. She sounded worried."

"Egg, my dear, what do I care for Miss Milray's worries? What do I care for anything but today? Let murder go hang."

They arrived back at Sir Charles's flat for tea. Miss Milray came out to meet them.

"There is a telegram for you, Sir Charles."

"Thank you, Miss Milray."

He tore it open and swung round with a quick exclamation: "Egg, look at this! It's from Satterthwaite!"

He shoved the telegram into her hands. Egg read it and her eyes opened wide.

CHAPTER XXV

BEFORE catching their train, Hercule Poirot and Mr. Satterthwaite had had a brief interview with Miss Lyndon, the late Sir Bartholomew Strange's secretary. Miss Lyndon had been very willing to help, but had had nothing of importance to tell them. Mrs. de Rushbridger was only mentioned in Sir Bartholomew's case book in a purely professional fashion. Sir Bartholomew had never spoken of her save in medical terms.

The two men arrived at the sanatorium about twelve o'clock. The maid who opened the door looked excited and flushed. Mr. Satterthwaite asked first for the matron.

"I don't know whether she can see you this morning," said the girl doubtfully.

Mr. Satterthwaite extracted a card and wrote a few words on it.

"Please take her this."

They were shown into a small waiting room. In about five minutes the door opened and the matron came in. She was looking quite unlike her usual brisk, efficient self.

Mr. Satterthwaite rose.

"I hope you remember me," he said. "I came here with Sir Charles Cartwright just after the death of Sir Bartholomew Strange."

"Yes, indeed, Mr. Satterthwaite, of course I remember, and Sir Charles asked after poor Mrs. de Rushbridger then, and it seems such a coincidence."

"Let me introduce M. Hercule Poirot."

Poirot bowed and the matron responded absently. She went on:

170

"I can't understand how you can have had a telegram, as you say. The whole thing seems most mysterious. Surely it can't be connected with the poor doctor's death in any way. There must be some madman about—that's the only way I can account for it. Having the police here and everything. It's really been terrible."

"The police?" said Mr. Satterthwaite, surprised.

"Yes, since ten o'clock they've been here."

"The police?" said Hercule Poirot.

"Perhaps we could see Mrs. de Rushbridger now," suggested Mr. Satterthwaite. "Since she asked us to come."

The matron interrupted him:

"Oh, Mr. Satterthwaite, then you don't know!"

"Know what?" demanded Poirot sharply.

"Poor Mrs. de Rushbridger. She's dead."

"Dead?" cried Poirot. *"Mille tonnerres!* That explains it. Yes, that explains it. I should have seen——" He broke off. "How did she die?"

"It's most mysterious. A box of chocolates came for her— liqueur chocolates—by post. She ate one; it must have tasted horrible, but she was taken by surprise, I suppose, and she swallowed it. One doesn't like spitting a thing out."

"Oui, oui, and if a liquid runs suddenly down your throat, it is difficult."

"So she swallowed it and called out, and nurse came rushing, but we couldn't do anything. She died in about two minutes. Then doctor sent for the police, and they came and examined the chocolates. All the top layer had been tampered with; the underneath ones were all right."

"And the poison employed?"

"They think it's nicotine."

"Yes," said Poirot. "Again nicotine. What a stroke! What an audacious stroke!"

"We are too late," said Mr. Satterthwaite. "We shall never know now what she had to tell us. Unless—unless she confided in someone?" He glanced interrogatively at the matron.

Poirot shook his head. "There will have been no confidence, you will find."

"We can ask," said Mr. Satterthwaite. "One of the nurses, perhaps?"

"By all means ask," said Poirot, but he did not sound hopeful.

Mr. Satterthwaite turned to the matron, who immediately sent for the two nurses, on day and night duty respectively, who had been in attendance on Mrs. de Rushbridger, but neither of them could add any information to that already given. Mrs. de Rushbridger had never mentioned Sir Bartholomew's death, and they did not even know of the dispatching of the telegram.

On a request from Poirot, the two men were taken to the dead woman's room. They found Superintendent Crossfield in charge, and Mr. Satterthwaite introduced him to Poirot.

Then the two men moved over to the bed and stood looking down on the dead woman. She was about forty, dark-haired and pale. Her face was not peaceful; it still showed the agony of her death.

Mr. Satterthwaite said slowly:

"Poor soul."

He looked across at Hercule Poirot. There was a strange expression on the little Belgian's face. Something about it made Mr. Satterthwaite shiver.

Mr. Satterthwaite said:

"Someone knew she was going to speak and killed her. She was killed in order to prevent her speaking."

Poirot nodded.

"Yes, that is so."

"She was murdered to prevent her telling us what she knew."

"Or what she did not know. But let us not waste time. There is much to be done. There must be no more deaths. We must see to that."

Mr. Satterthwaite asked curiously:

"Does this fit in with your idea of the murderer's identity?"

"Yes, it fits. But I realize one thing: The murderer is more dangerous than I thought. We must be careful."

Superintendent Crossfield followed them out of the room and learned from them of the telegram which had been received by them. The telegram had been handed in at Melfort Post Office, and on inquiry there, it was elicited that it had been handed in by a small boy. The young lady in charge remembered it, because the message had excited her very much, mentioning, as it did, Sir Bartholomew Strange's death.

After some lunch in company with the superintendent, and after dispatching a telegram to Sir Charles, the quest was resumed.

At six o'clock that evening, the small boy who had handed in the telegram was found. He told his story promptly. He had been given the telegram by a man dressed in shabby clothes. The man told him that the telegram had been given him by a "loony lady" in the "house in the park." She had dropped it out of the window wrapped round two half crowns. The man was afraid to be mixed up in some funny business, and was tramping in the other direction, so he had given the boy two and six, and told him to keep the change.

A search would be instituted for the man. In the meantime there seemed nothing more to be done, and Poirot and Mr. Satterthwaite returned to London.

It was close on midnight when the two men arrived back in town. Egg had gone back to her mother, but Sir Charles met them and the three men discussed the situation.

"*Mon ami,*" said Poirot, "be guided by me. Only one thing will solve this case—the little gray cells of the brain. To rush up and down England, to hope that this person and that will tell us what we want to know—all such methods are amateurish and absurd. The truth can only be seen from within."

Sir Charles looked slightly skeptical.

"What do you want to do, then?"

"I want to think. I ask of you twenty-four hours in which to think."

Sir Charles shook his head with a slight smile.

"Will thinking tell you what it was that this woman could have said if she lived?"

"I believe so."

"It hardly seems possible. However, M. Poirot, you must have it your own way. If you can see through this mystery, it's more than I can. I'm beaten, and I confess it. In any case, I've other fish to fry."

Perhaps he hoped to be questioned, but if so, his expectation was disappointed. Mr. Satterthwaite did indeed look up alertly, but Poirot remained lost in thought.

"Well, I must be off," said the actor. . . . "Oh, just one thing. I'm rather worried about Miss Wills."

"What about her?"

"She's gone."

"Poirot stared at him.

"Gone? Gone where?"

"Nobody knows. I was thinking things over after I got your telegram. As I told you at the time, I felt convinced that that woman knew something she hadn't told us. I thought I'd have a last shot at getting it out of her. I drove out to her house—it was about half-past nine when I got there—and asked for her. It appears she left home this morning—went up to London for the day—that's what she said. Her people got a telegram in the evening, saying she wasn't returning for a day or so, and not to worry."

"And were they worrying?"

"I gather they were, rather. You see, she hadn't taken any luggage with her."

"Odd," murmured Poirot.

"I know. It seems as though—— I don't know. I feel uneasy."

"I warned her," said Poirot. "I warned everyone. You remember, I said to them, 'Speak now.'"

"Yes, yes. Do you think that she too——"

"I have my ideas," said Poirot. "For the moment, I prefer not to discuss them."

"First the butler, Ellis, then Miss Wills. Where is Ellis? It's incredible that the police have never been able to lay hands on him."

"They have not looked for his body in the right place," said Poirot.

"Then you agree with Egg. You think that he is dead?"

"Ellis will never be seen alive again."

"It's a nightmare!" burst out Sir Charles. "The whole thing is utterly incomprehensible!"

"No, no. It is sane and logical, on the contrary."

Sir Charles stared at him.

"You say that?"

"Certainly. You see, I have the orderly mind."

"I don't understand you."

Mr. Satterthwaite, too, looked curiously at the little detective.

"What kind of a mind have I?" demanded Sir Charles, slightly hurt.

"You have the actor's mind, Sir Charles, creative, original, seeing always dramatic values. Mr. Satterthwaite here, he has the playgoer's mind; he observes the characters, he has the sense of atmosphere. But me, I have the prosaic mind. I see only the facts, without any dramatic trappings or footlights."

"Then we're to leave you to it?"

"That is my idea. For twenty-four hours."

"Good luck to you, then. Good night."

As they went away together, Sir Charles said to Mr. Satterthwaite:

"That chap thinks a lot of himself."

He spoke rather coldly.

CHAPTER XXVI

POIROT did not have quite the uninterrupted twenty-four hours for which he had stipulated.

It was a little after ten on the following morning when Oliver Manders sent up his card and asked if M. Poirot could spare him a few moments.

When Manders entered the room, Poirot was in the act of unwrapping a small parcel. He laid it aside and looked inquiringly at his visitor.

"Good morning, M. Manders," he said. "You wished to see me?"

"Yes."

Oliver hesitated. Poirot drew forward a chair.

"Sit, I pray of you.... Now we can converse at our ease."

Oliver accepted the chair, but he still seemed a little doubtful as how best to come to the point of his visit.

"*Eh bien?*" said Poirot. "What is it that you seek? Do you come to render me a service? Or is it that you want me to do you one?"

"I don't know," said Oliver slowly.

Then suddenly he leaned forward and said impulsively:

"M. Poirot, you don't like me."

Poirot looked slightly astonished.

"But what an idea—that."

"No, you don't like me. Very few people do like me. I—I don't know why it is."

All Oliver's languid, supercilious manner had vanished. He spoke now as boyishly and naturally as any other young man of his age might have done. His face, as he leaned forward, had lost its usual sneering expression. It showed instead a diffidence and an eagerness that were somehow a little pathetic.

"But why should you think I do not like you?" asked Poirot gently.

"Because the day before yesterday, when you staged that mock murder, it was—it was a trap for me."

Again Poirot's eyebrows rose.

"How so?"

Oliver replied somberly:

"Because in the bottom of your heart you believe that it was I who killed old Babbington."

"*Quelle idée!*"

"No, you think so. I can see that there is a lot against me, but I'm not a murderer, M. Poirot. I'm not! I was rude to the old fellow once—very rude—but if you'll believe me, I felt miserable about it afterwards. It's as though there were two of me. One's a hateful drawling sneering sort of chap, always posing. The other's not like that, but he finds it hard to show himself. Oh, you can't understand what I mean."

"Yes, yes, I understand very well. Because I am old, I have not forgotten what it is to be young." He went on gently: "That is your complaint, *mon ami*—youth. It is a characteristic of youth to make itself out worse than it is." With a slightly humorous grimace, he added: "At my age, one's preoccupation is to arrange one's goods well in the shop window."

"You understand, then?" Oliver looked grateful. A really charming smile came over his face. "You don't know what a difference it makes if someone's willing to make the best of you, and not the worst."

"You have not had the life very happy, eh?"

Oliver's face hardened.

"No."

"Listen; now I will give you advice. Your life is your own, to make of what you will. Bitterness leads nowhere. It turns back on itself. It is the eternal cul-de-sac. Put it away from you now, before it is too late."

"You're right, M. Poirot. I'm going to put everything behind me and start afresh."

"Good."

Poirot nodded approval, and then went on: "And the next thing?"

Oliver looked rather surprised.

"The next thing?"

"*Mais oui.* I fancied you had something else to say, but perhaps I am wrong."

"No, no, you're right. There is something more. I want you to let me work with you over this business. You trust me now. Let me help you."

"Help me? In what way?"

"I don't know. There must be some way in which I could be useful. I fancy—I may be wrong—that you are very hot on the trail."

He waited rather breathlessly for Poirot's answer, which was a little slow in coming.

"It is possible," he said, "that you may be able to help me, soon."

"Oh, I say, that's grand."

Oliver waited a minute or two, but Poirot said no more.

"If you could just tell me the way your suspicions are pointing——"

Hercule Poirot shook his head.

"That—not just yet. I am of an unbelievable secrecy."

Oliver's ear was sensitive enough to catch the underlying firmness in Poirot's voice. He insisted no further, but took his leave with a few further words of thanks.

There was a strange smile on Poirot's face as young Oliver Manders left the room.

He murmured to himself, "I underrated that young man."

Then he picked up his half-unwrapped package.

It was twenty minutes past eleven when Egg walked in unannounced. To her amazement, she found the great detective engaged in building card houses.

Her face showed such lively scorn that Poirot was impelled to defend himself.

"It is not, mademoiselle, that I have become childish in my old age. No. But the building of card houses, I have always found it most stimulating to the mind. It is an old habit of mine. This morning, first thing, I go out and buy the pack of cards. Unfortunately, I make an error; they are not real cards. But they do just as well."

Egg looked more closely at the erection on the table. She laughed.

"Good heavens, they've sold you Happy Families."

"What is that you say—the Happy Family?"

"Yes, it's a game. Children play it in the nursery."

"Ah, well, one can compose the houses just in the same manner."

Egg had picked up some of the cards from the table and was looking at them affectionately.

"Master Bun, the baker's son—I always loved him. And here's Mr. Mug, the milkman. Oh, dear, I wish Sir Charles were here. I'd show him his portrait."

"Why is that funny picture Sir Charles, mademoiselle?"

"Because of the name."

Egg laughed at his bewildered face, and then began explaining. When she had finished, he said:

"*Ah, ç'est ca.* Cartwright, it is the *nom de théatre.* Mugg—ah, yes, one says in slang, does not one, you are a mug—a fool? Naturally, you would change your name. One would not like to be Sir Charles Mugg, eh?"

Egg laughed. She said:

"To be Lady Mugg would be worse."

Poirot looked at her keenly and she blushed.

"*C'est comme ça?*"

"Not at all," said Egg. "I don't know what you mean." She went on quickly: "This is what I came to see you about. I've been worrying and worrying about that cutting from the paper that Oliver dropped from his wallet. You know, the one Miss Wills picked up and handed back to him. It seems to me that either Oliver is telling a downright lie when he says he doesn't remember its being there, or else it never was there. He dropped some odd bit of paper and that woman pretended it was the nicotine cutting."

"Why should she have done that, mademoiselle?"

"Because she wanted to get rid of it. She planted it on Oliver."

"You mean she is the criminal?"

"Yes."

"What was her motive?"

"It's no good asking me that. I can only suggest that she's a lunatic. Clever people often are rather mad. I can't see any other reason—in fact, I can't see any motive anywhere."

179

"Decidedly, that is the *impasse*. I should not ask you to guess at a motive. It is of myself that I ask that question without ceasing: What was the motive behind Mr. Babbington's death? When I can answer that, the case will be solved."

"You don't think just madness——" suggested Egg.

"There must still be a motive—a mad motive, if you like, but a motive. That is what I seek."

"Well, good-bye," said Egg. "I'm sorry to have disturbed you, but the idea just occurred to me. I must hurry. I'm going with Charles to the dress rehearsal of *Little Dog Laughed*—you know, the play Miss Wills has written for Angela Sutcliffe. It's the first night tomorrow."

"Mon Dieu!" cried Poirot.

"What is it? Has anything happened?"

"Yes, indeed, something has happened. An idea. A superb idea. Oh, but I have been blind—blind."

Egg stared at him. As though realizing his eccentricity, Poirot took a hold on himself. He patted Egg on the shoulder.

"You think I am mad. Not at all. I heard what you said. You go to see the *Little Dog Laughed* and Miss Sutcliffe acts in it. Go then, and pay no attention to what I have said."

Rather doubtfully, Egg departed. Left to himself, Poirot strode up and down the room muttering under his breath. His eyes shone green as any cat's.

"Mais oui, that explains everything. A curious motive—a very curious motive—such a motive as I have never come across before, and yet it is reasonable and, given the circumstances, natural. Altogether it is a very curious case."

He passed the table where his card house still reposed. With a sweep of his hands he swept the cards from the table.

"The Happy Family, I need it no longer," he said. "The problem is solved. It only remains to act."

He caught up his hat and put on his overcoat. Then he went downstairs and the commissionaire called him a taxi. Poirot gave the address of Sir Charles's flat.

Arrived there, he paid off the taxi and stepped into the hall. The porter was absent, taking up the lift. Poirot walked up the stairs. Just as he arrived on the second floor, the door of Sir Charles's flat opened and Miss Milray came out.

She started when she saw Poirot.

"You!"

Poirot smiled.

"Me! Or is it I? *Enfin, moi!*"

Miss Milray said:

"I'm afraid you won't find Sir Charles. He's gone to the Babylon Theater with Miss Lytton Gore."

"It is not Sir Charles I seek. It is my stick that I think I have left behind one day."

"Oh, I see. Well, if you'll ring, Temple will find it for you. I'm sorry I can't stop. I'm on my way to catch a train. I'm going to the country to see my mother."

"I comprehend. Do not let me delay you, mademoiselle."

He stood aside and Miss Milray passed rapidly down the stairs. She was carrying a small attaché case.

But when she had gone, Poirot seemed to forget the purpose for which he had come. Instead of going on up to the landing, he turned and made his way downstairs again. He arrived at the front door just in time to see Miss Milray getting into a taxi. Another taxi was coming slowly along the curb. Poirot raised a hand and it came to rest. He got in and directed the driver to follow the other taxi.

No surprise showed on his face when the first taxi went north and finally drew up at Paddington Station, though Paddington is an odd station from which to proceed to Gilling. Poirot went to the first-class booking window and demanded a return ticket to Loomouth. The train was due to depart in five minutes. Pulling up his overcoat well about his ears, for the day was cold, Poirot ensconced himself in the corner of a first-class carriage.

They arrived at Loomouth about five o'clock. It was already growing dark. Standing back a little, Poirot heard Miss Milray being greeted by the friendly porter at the little station:

"Well, now, miss, we didn't expect you. Is Sir Charles coming down?"

Miss Milray replied:

"I've come down here unexpectedly. I shall be going back tomorrow morning. I've just come to fetch some things. No, I don't want a cab, thank you. I'll walk up by the cliff path."

The dusk had deepened. Miss Milray walked briskly up the steep zigzag path. A good way behind came Hercule Poirot. He trod softly, like a cat. Miss Milray, on arrival at Crow's

Nest, produced a key from her bag and passed through the side door, leaving it ajar. She reappeared a minute or two later. She had a rusty door key and an electric torch in her hand. Poirot drew back a little behind a convenient bush.

Miss Milray passed round behind the house and up a scrambling, overgrown path. Hercule Poirot followed. Up and up went Miss Milray, until she came suddenly to an old stone tower such as is found often on that coast. This one was of humble and dilapidated appearance. There was, however, a curtain over the dirty window, and Miss Milray inserted her key in the big wooden door.

The key turned with a protesting creak. The door swung with a groan on its hinges. Miss Milray and her torch passed inside.

With an increase of pace, Poirot caught up. He passed, in his turn, noiselessly through the door. The light of Miss Milray's torch gleamed fitfully on glass—retorts, a Bunsen burner, various apparatus.

Miss Milray had picked up a crowbar. She had raised it and was holding it over the glass apparatus when a hand caught her by the arm. She gasped and turned.

The green, catlike eyes of Hercule Poirot looked into hers.

"You cannot do that, mademoiselle," he said. "For what you seek to destroy is evidence."

CHAPTER XXVII

HERCULE Poirot sat in a big armchair. The wall lights had been turned out. Only a rose-shaded lamp shed its glow on the figure in the armchair. There seemed something symbolic about it—he alone in the light, and the other three, Sir Charles, Mr. Satterthwaite and Egg Lytton Gore—Poirot's audience— sitting in the outer darkness.

Hercule Poirot's voice was dreamy. He seemed to be addressing himself to space rather than to his listeners:

"To reconstruct the crime—that is the aim of the detective. To reconstruct a crime, you must place one fact upon another just as you place one card on another in building a house of cards. And if the facts will not fit—if the card will not balance—well, you must start your house again, or else it will fall.

"As I said the other day, there are different types of minds; there is the dramatic mind, the producer's mind, which sees the effect of reality that can be produced by mechanical appliances; there is also the mind that reacts easily to dramatic appearances; and there is the young romantic mind; and finally, my friends, there is the prosaic mind—the mind that sees, not blue sea and mimosa trees, but the painted backcloth of stage scenery.

"So I come, *mes amis*, to the murder of Stephen Babbington in August last. On that evening, Sir Charles Cartwright advanced the theory that Stephen Babbington had been murdered. I did not agree with that theory. I could not believe (A) that such a man as Stephen Babbington was likely to have been murdered, and (B) that it was possible to administer

183

poison to a particular person under the circumstances that had obtained that evening.

"Now, here I admit that Sir Charles was right and I was wrong. I was wrong because I was looking at the crime from an entirely false angle. It is only twenty-four hours ago that I suddenly perceived the proper angle of vision—and let me say that from that angle of vision, the murder of Stephen Babbington is both reasonable and possible.

"But I will pass from that point for the moment and take you step by step along the path I myself have trodden. The death of Stephen Babbington I may call the first act of our drama. The curtain fell on that act when we all departed from Crow's Nest.

"What I might call the second act of the drama began in Monte Carlo, when Mr. Satterthwaite showed me the newspaper account of Sir Bartholomew's death. It was at once clear that I had been wrong and Sir Charles had been right. Both Stephen Babbington and Sir Bartholomew Strange had been murdered, and the two murders formed part of one and the same crime. Later, a third murder completed the series— the murder of Mrs. de Rushbridger.

"What we need, therefore, is a reasonable commonsense theory which will link those three deaths together—in other words, those three crimes were committed by one and the same person and were to the advantage and benefit of that particular person.

"Now, I may say at once that the principal thing that worried me was the fact that the murder of Sir Bartholomew Strange came after that of Stephen Babbington. Looking at those three murders without distinction of time and place, the probabilities pointed to the murder of Sir Bartholomew Strange being what one might call the central or principal crime, and the two other murders as secondary in character— that is, arising from the connection of those two people with Sir Bartholomew Strange. However, as I remarked before, one cannot have one's crime as one would like to have it. Stephen Babbington had been murdered first and Sir Bartholomew Strange some time later. It seemed, therefore, as though the second crime must necessarily arise out of the first, and that, accordingly, it was the first crime we must examine for the clue to the whole.

"I did indeed so far incline to the theory of probability that I seriously considered the idea of a mistake having arisen. Was it possible that Sir Bartholomew Strange was intended as the first victim and that Mr. Babbington was poisoned by mistake? I was forced, however, to abandon that idea. Anybody who knew Sir Bartholomew Strange with any degree of intimacy knew that he disliked the cocktail habit.

"Another suggestion: Had Stephen Babbington been poisoned in mistake for any other member of the original party? I could not find any evidence of such a thing. I was therefore forced back to the conclusion that the murder of Stephen Babbington had been definitely intended, and at once I came up against a complete stumbling-block—the apparent impossibility of such a thing having happened.

"One should always start an investigation with the simplest and most obvious theories. Granting that Stephen Babbington had drunk a poisoned cocktail, who had had the opportunity of poisoning that cocktail? At first sight, it seemed to me that the only two people who could have done so—for example, those who handled the drinks—were Sir Charles Cartwright himself and the parlormaid, Temple. But though either of them could presumably have introduced the poison into the glass, neither of them had had any opportunity of directing that particular glass into Mr. Babbington's hand. Temple might have done so by adroit handing of the tray so as to offer him the one remaining glass—not easy, but it might have been done. Sir Charles could have done so by deliberately picking up the particular glass and handing it to him. But neither of these things had occurred. It looked as though chance, and chance alone, directed that particular glass to Stephen Babbington.

"Sir Charles Cartwright and Temple had the handling of the cocktails. Were either of those two at Melfort Abbey? They were not. Who had the best chance of tampering with Sir Bartholomew's port glass? The absconding butler, Ellis, and his helper, the parlormaid. But here, however, the possibility that one of the guests had done so could not be laid aside. It was risky, but it was possible, for any of the house party to have slipped into the dining room and put the nicotine into the port glass.

"When I joined you at Crow's Nest, you already had a list

drawn up of the people who had been at Crow's Nest and at Melfort Abbey. I may say now, that the four names which headed the list—Captain and Mrs. Dacres, Miss Sutcliffe and Miss Wills—I discarded immediately.

"It was impossible that any of those four people should have known beforehand that they were going to meet Stephen Babbington at dinner. The employment of nicotine as a poison showed a carefully thought-out plan, not one that could be put into operation on the spur of the moment. There were three other names on that list—Lady Mary Lytton Gore, Miss Lytton Gore and Mr. Oliver Manders. Although not probable, those three were possible. They were local people; they might conceivably have motives for the removal of Stephen Babbington and have chosen the evening of the dinner party for putting their plans into operation.

"On the other hand, I could find no evidence whatsoever that any one of them had actually done such a thing.

"Mr. Satterthwaite, I think, reasoned on much the same lines as I had done, and he fixed his suspicions on Oliver Manders. I may say that young Manders was by far the most possible suspect. He displayed all the signs of high nervous tension on that evening at Crow's Nest; he had a somewhat distorted view of life owing to his private troubles; he had a strong inferiority complex, which is a frequent cause of crime; he was at an unbalanced age; he had actually had a quarrel, or shall we say, had displayed animosity against Mr. Babbington. Then there were the curious circumstances of his arrival at Melfort Abbey. And later we had his somewhat incredible story of the letter from Sir Bartholomew Strange and the newspaper cutting on the subject of nicotine poisoning in his possession. There was also the reference to M in Sir Bartholomew's diary.

"Oliver Manders, then, was clearly the person who should be placed at the head of the list of those seven suspects.

"But then, my friends, I was visited by a curious sensation. It seemed clear and logical enough that the person who had committed the crimes must have been a person who had been present on both occasions—in other words, a person on that list of seven—but I had the feeling that that obviousness was an arranged obviousness. It was what any sane and logical person would be expected to think. That I was, in fact, looking not at reality but at an artfully painted bit of scenery. A really clever criminal would have realized that anyone whose name was on that list would necessarily be suspect, and therefore he or she would arrange for it not to be there.

"In other words, the murderer of Stephen Babbington and Sir Bartholomew Strange was present on both occasions, but was not apparently so.

"Who had been present on the first occasion and not on the second? Sir Charles Cartwright, Mr. Satterthwaite, Miss Milray and Mrs. Babbington.

"Could any of those four have been present on the second occasion in some capacity other than their own? Sir Charles and Mr. Satterthwaite had been in the South of France, Miss Milray had been in London, Mrs. Babbington had been in Loomouth. Of the four, then, Miss Milray and Mrs. Babbington seemed indicated. But could Miss Milray have been present at Melfort Abbey unrecognized by any of the company? Miss Milray has very striking features, not easily disguised and not easily forgotten. I decided that it was impossible that Miss Milray could have been at Melfort Abbey unrecognized. The same applied to Mrs. Babbington.

"For the matter of that, could Mr. Satterthwaite or Sir Charles Cartwright have been at Melfort Abbey and not been recognized? Mr. Satterthwaite just possibly, but when we come to Sir Charles Cartwright, we come to a very different matter. Sir Charles is an actor accustomed to playing a part. But what part could he have played?

"And then I came to the consideration of the butler, Ellis.

"A very mysterious person, Ellis. A person who appears from nowhere a fortnight before the crime and vanishes afterward with complete success. Why was Ellis so successful? Because Ellis did not really exist. Ellis, again, was a thing of pasteboard and paint and stagecraft; Ellis was not real.

"But was it possible? After all, the servants at Melfort Abbey knew Sir Charles Cartwright, and Sir Bartholomew Strange was an intimate friend of his. The servants I got over easily enough. The impersonation of the butler risked nothing; if the servants recognized him—why, no harm would be done—the whole thing could be passed off as a joke. If, on the other hand, a fortnight passed without any suspicion being aroused—well, the thing was safe as houses. And I recalled what I had been told of the servants' remarks about the butler. He was 'quite the gentleman' and had been 'in good houses' and knew several interesting scandals. That was easy enough. But a very significant statement was made by the parlormaid, Doris. She said, 'He arranged the work different from any butler I ever knew before.' When that remark was repeated to me, it became a confirmation of my theory.

"But Sir Bartholomew Strange was another matter. It is hardly to be supposed that his friend could take him in. He must have known of the impersonation. Had we any evidence of that? Yes. The acute Mr. Satterthwaite pounced on one point quite early in the proceedings—the facetious remark of Sir Bartholomew; totally uncharacteristic of his manner to servants: 'You're a first-class butler, aren't you, Ellis?' A perfectly understandable remark if the butler were Sir Charles Cartwright and Sir Bartholomew was in on the joke.

"Because that is undoubtedly how Sir Bartholomew saw the matter. The impersonation of Ellis was a joke, possibly even a wager; its culmination was designed to be the successful spoofing of the house party; hence Sir Bartholomew's remark about a surprise and his cheerful humor. Note, too, that there was still time to draw back. If any of the house party had spotted Charles Cartwright that first evening at the dinner table, nothing irrevocable had yet occurred. The whole thing could have been passed off as a joke. But nobody noticed the stooping, middle-aged butler, with his belladonna-darkened eyes, and his whiskers, and the painted birthmark on his wrist. A very subtle identifying touch, that—which completely failed, owing to the lack of observation of most human beings. The birthmark was intended to bulk largely in the description of Ellis—and in all that fortnight no one noticed it! The only person who did was the sharp-eyed Miss Wills, to whom we shall come presently.

"What happened next? Sir Bartholomew died. This time the death was not put down to natural causes. The police came. They questioned Ellis and the others. Later that night Ellis left by the secret passage, resumed his own personality, and two days later was strolling about at Monte Carlo, ready to be shocked and surprised by the news of his friend's death.

"This, mind you, was all theory. I had no actual proof,

but everything that arose supported that theory. My house of cards was well and truly built. The blackmailing letters discovered in Ellis's room? But it was Sir Charles himself who discovered them!

"And what of the supposed letter from Sir Bartholomew Strange asking young Manders to arrange an accident? Well, what could be easier than for Sir Charles to write that letter in Sir Bartholomew's name? If Manders had not destroyed that letter himself, Sir Charles, in the rôle of Ellis, can easily do so when he valets the young gentleman. In the same way the newspaper cutting is easily introduced by Ellis into Oliver Manders's wallet.

"And now we come to the third victim—Mrs. de Rushbridger. When do we first hear of Mrs. de Rushbridger? Immediately after that very awkward, chaffing reference to Ellis being the perfect butler—that extremely uncharacteristic utterance of Sir Bartholomew Strange. At all costs, attention must be drawn away from Sir Bartholomew's manner to his butler. Sir Charles quickly asks what was the message the butler had brought. It is about this woman—this patient of the doctor's. And immediately Sir Charles throws all his personality into directing attention to this unknown woman and away from the butler. He goes to the sanatorium and questions the matron. He runs Mrs. de Rushbridger for all he is worth as a red herring.

"We must now examine the part played by Miss Wills in the drama. Miss Wills has a curious personality. She is one of those people who are quite unable to impress themselves on their surroundings. She is neither good-looking, nor witty, nor clever, nor even particularly sympathetic. She is nondescript. But she is extremely observant and extremely intelligent. She takes her revenge on the world with her pen. She has the great art of being able to reproduce character on paper. I do not know if there was anything about the butler that struck Miss Wills as unusual, but I do think that she was the only person at the table who noticed him at all. On the morning after the murder, her insatiable curiosity led her to poke and pry, as the housemaid put it. She went into Dacres's room; she went through the baize door into the servants' quarters; led, I think, by the mongoose instinct for finding out.

"She was the only person who occasioned Sir Charles any

uneasiness. That is why he was anxious to be the one to tackle her. He was fairly reassured by his interview and distinctly gratified that she had noticed the birthmark. But after that came catastrophe. I don't think that until that minute Miss Wills had connected Ellis, the butler, with Sir Charles Cartwright. I think she had only been vaguely struck by some resemblance to someone in Ellis. But she was an observer. When dishes were handed to her, she had automatically noted, not the face, but the hands that held the dishes.

"It did not occur to her that Ellis was Sir Charles. But when Sir Charles was talking to her, it did suddenly occur to her that Sir Charles was Ellis! And so she asked him to pretend to hand her a dish of vegetables. But it was not whether the birthmark was on the right or left wrist that interested her. She wanted a pretext to study his hands— hands held in the same position as those of Ellis, the butler.

"And so she leaped to the truth. But she was a peculiar woman. She enjoyed knowledge for its own sake. Besides, she was by no means sure that Sir Charles had murdered his friend. He had masqueraded as a butler, yes; but that did not necessarily make him a murderer. Many an innocent man has kept silence because speech would place him in an awkward position.

"So Miss Wills kept her knowledge to herself, and enjoyed it. But Sir Charles was worried. He did not like that expression of satisfied malice on her face that he saw as he left the room. She knew something. What? Did it affect him? He could not be sure. But he felt that it was something connected with Ellis, the butler. First Mr. Satterthwaite, now Miss Wills. Attention must be drawn away from that vital point. It must be focused away from that vital point. It must be focused definitely elsewhere. And he thought of a plan— simple, audacious and, as he fancied, definitely mystifying.

"On the day of my sherry party, I imagine Sir Charles rose very early, went to Yorkshire, and, disguised in shabby clothes, gave the telegram to a small boy to send off. Then he returned to town in time to act the part I had indicated in my little drama. He did one more thing. He posted a box of chocolates to a woman he had never seen and of whom he knew nothing.

"You know what happened that evening. From Sir Charles's

uneasiness, I was fairly sure that Miss Wills had certain suspicions. When Sir Charles did his death scene, I watched Miss Wills's face. I saw the look of astonishment that showed on it. I knew then that Miss Wills definitely suspected Sir Charles of being the murderer. When he appeared to die, poisoned, like the other two, she thought her deductions must be wrong.

"But if Miss Wills suspected Sir Charles, then Miss Wills was in serious danger. A man who has killed twice will kill again. I uttered a very solemn warning. Later that night I communicated with Miss Wills by telephone, and on my advice she left home suddenly the next day. Since then she has been living here in this hotel. That I was wise is proved by the fact that Sir Charles went out to Tooting on the following evening after he had returned from Gilling. He was too late. The bird had flown.

"In the meantime, from his point of view, the plan had worked well. Mrs. de Rushbridger had something of importance to tell us. Mrs. de Rushbridger was killed before she could speak. How dramatic! How like the detective stories, the plays, the films! Again the cardboard and the tinsel and the painted cloth.

"But I, Hercule Poirot, was not deceived. Mr. Satterthwaite said to me that she was killed in order that she should not speak. I agreed. He went on to say that she was killed before she could tell us what she knew. I said: 'Or what she did not know.' I think he was puzzled. But he should have seen, then, the truth. Mrs. de Rushbridger was killed because she could, in actual fact, have told us nothing at all. Because she had no connection with the crime. If she were to be Sir Charles's successful red herring, she could only be so, dead. And so Mrs. de Rushbridger, a harmless stranger, was murdered.

"Yet even in that seeming triumph, Sir Charles made a colossal—a childish error! The telegram was addressed to me, Hercule Poirot, at the Ritz Hotel. But Mrs. de Rushbridger had never heard of my connection with the case! No one up in that part of the world knew of it. It was an unbelievably childish error.

"*Eh bien,* then, I had reached a certain stage. I knew the

identity of the murderer. But I did not know the motive for
the original crime.

I reflected.

"And once again, more clearly than ever, I saw the death
of Sir Bartholomew Strange as the original and purposeful
murder. What reason could Sir Charles Cartwright have for
the murder of his friend? Could I imagine a motive? I thought
I could."

There was a deep sigh. Sir Charles Cartwright rose slowly
to his feet and strolled to the fireplace. He stood there, his
hand on his hip, looking down at Poirot. His attitude, Mr.
Satterthwaite could have told you, was that of Lord Englemount
as he looks scornfully at the rascally solicitor who has succeeded in fastening an accusation of fraud upon him. He
radiated nobility and disgust. He was the aristocrat looking
down at the ignoble *canaille*.

"You have an extraordinary imagination, M. Poirot," he
said. "It's hardly worthwhile saying that there's not one
single word of truth in your story. How you have the damned
impertinence to dish up such an absurd fandangle of lies, I
don't know. But go on; I am interested. What was my motive
for murdering a man whom I had known ever since boyhood?"

Hercule Poirot, the little bourgeois, looked up at the
aristocrat. He spoke quietly, but firmly:

"Sir Charles, there are not so very many motives for
murder. There is fear, there is gain, there is—a woman. In
your case, Sir Charles, we need not look beyond the first of
these. Your motive for murdering Sir Bartholomew Strange
was fear."

Sir Charles shrugged a disdainful shoulder.

"And why had I any reason to fear my old friend?"

"Because," said Hercule Poirot, "Sir Bartholomew was a
mental specialist."

He paused for a moment, then went on in a gentle, re-
mote voice:

"Since this idea came to me, I have made inquiries. I
have looked up the files of newspapers. Perhaps, Sir Charles,
you remember mentioning before Mr. Satterthwaite that you
had abandoned your career after a nervous breakdown occasioned by overwork. That statement fell somewhat short of
the real truth. I note that in the last two years of your stage

career you acted in three plays—one a dramatized version of the life of Napoleon, the second a religious pastoral play in which your part was that of the Deity dimly disguised, and the third a crook play in which you acted the rôle of a super-dictator who mastered the world. In your public speeches at that time there are undoubted traces of egomania. As to your actual breakdown, the details are very vague. It was announced in the press that you had gone on a cruise. But I failed to find your name in any of the passenger lists of likely shipping companies.

"Unwittingly, at this stage Miss Lytton Gore came to my help. She let fall the fact that your real name was Mugg, and immediately a sentence sprang into my mind—that sentence penciled in Sir Bartholomew's diary: 'Am worried about M. Don't like the look of things.' M stood not for Manders, nor for Margaret de Rushbridger, nor for some person unknown. M stood for Mugg— the name under which Sir Bartholomew knew you as a young man. And very speedily I found confirmation of my theory. On the date on which Sir Charles was supposed to have set off on a cruise, a patient named Charles Mugg was admitted to a private mental home in Lincolnshire. I can understand the reasons for such a procedure—Sir Charles Cartwright was well known to the staff of Sir Bartholomew's sanatorium at the abbey. This method avoided all publicity. Charles Mugg was discharged from the home in question after a stay of four months, but I can imagine that the doctor was not wholly satisfied about his friend's mental condition. And no doubt his watchful attitude precipitated the tragedy.

"Sir Charles's malady was not cured; he merely concealed it very cunningly from the world. But he was less sure of concealing it from the anxious and experienced eyes of his friend. And so, while Sir Bartholomew was no more than vaguely dissatisfied with his friend's mental condition, Sir Charles was laying his plans with the cunning natural to his state of mind.

"In Sir Bartholomew he saw a menace to his freedom. He was convinced that Sir Bartholomew was planning to put him under restraint. And so he planned a careful and extremely cunning murder.

"One thing had puzzled me all along—the relations between Sir Charles and Miss Lytton Gore. To Mr. Satterthwaite, he pretended to be the dense lover who cannot recognize his mistress's answering passion. He pretended to think that Miss Lytton Gore was in love with Mr. Oliver Manders. But I say that a man like Sir Charles—a man with a great knowledge of the world, and an experienced man where women are concerned—could not possibly have been so deceived. He must have known that he had a clear field. How, then, explain his attitude?

"Very simply. Sir Charles wanted an excuse to leave Loomouth and go abroad. He wanted an excuse that would reasonably explain his avoiding his friends for a while. And with that genius for dramatic effect which is undoubtedly his, he saw that nothing would be so effective as a romantic reason. It made him stand out at once as a sympathetic figure. It gave him, too, an excuse for returning to England after the death of Sir Bartholomew Strange and for taking part in the investigation. It was vital to him to know just how things were going."

Hercule Poirot paused.

Sir Charles laughed. It was a hearty, deeply amused laugh.

"My dear fellow," he said. "Really, my dear fellow."

And had there been an audience sitting in the stalls, they would have felt that really this absurd foreigner's ideas were too ridiculous. Sir Charles fairly radiated sanity.

"So I'm mad, am I?" said Sir Charles, with great good humor. "My dear M. Poirot, are you sure the boot is not on the other leg? We won't say senile decay, but"—he touched his forehead—"just a shade ga-ga, in my opinion. I admit my nerves were all to pieces, and on Tollie's advice I went to a private nursing home for a bit. But to regard me as a homicidal maniac—well, that's a bit too much."

He paused and then went on, still in the same tone of good-humored amusement:

"And Babbington—that dear old clergyman? Was he, too, an authority on insanity?"

"No," said Hercule Poirot. "The reason for the removal of Mr. Babbington was quite a different one. There was, in fact, no reason."

"Just a little homicidal fun, in fact?"

"No, there was more to it than that. All along I have been

held up by the fact that though on that evening you had a full opportunity for putting the nicotine into the cocktail glass, you could not have insured its reaching one particular person. Yesterday, through a chance remark, I saw light. The poison was not intended specially for Stephen Babbington. It was intended for anyone present, with the exception of two people— yourself and Sir Bartholomew, who, you knew, did not drink cocktails."

Mr. Satterthwaite cried out:

"But that's nonsense! What's the point of it? There isn't any."

Poirot turned toward him. Triumph came into his voice:

"Oh, yes, there is. A queer point—a very queer point. The only time I have come across such a motive for murder. The murder of Stephen Babbington was neither more nor less than a dress rehearsal."

"What?"

"Yes, Sir Charles was an actor. He obeyed his actor's instinct. He tried out his murder before committing it. No suspicion could possibly attach to him. Not one of those people's deaths could benefit him in any way and, moreover, as everyone has found, he could not have been proved to have poisoned any particular person. And, my friends, the dress rehearsal went well. Mr. Babbington dies, and foul play is not even suspected. It is left to Sir Charles to urge that suspicion, and he is highly gratified at our refusal to take it seriously. The substitution of the glass, too—that has gone without a hitch. In fact, he can be sure that, when the real performance comes, it will be 'all right on the night.'

"As you know, events took a slightly different turn. On the second occasion a doctor was present who immediately suspected poison. It was then to Sir Charles's interests to stress the death of Babbington. Sir Bartholomew's death must be presumed to be the outcome of that earlier death. Attention must be focused on the motive for Babbington's murder, not on any motive that might exist for Sir Bartholomew's removal.

"But there was one thing that Sir Charles failed to realize. The efficient watchfulness of Miss Milray. Miss Milray knew that her employer dabbled in chemical experiments in the tower in the garden. Miss Milray paid bills for rose-spraying solution and realized that quite a lot of it had unaccountably disappeared. When she read that Mr. Babbington had died of nicotine poisoning, her clever brain leaped at once to the conclusion that Sir Charles had extracted the pure alkaloid from the rose solution.

"And Miss Milray did not know what to do, for she had known Mr. Babbington as a little girl, and she was in love, deeply and devotedly as an ugly woman can be, with her fascinating employer.

"In the end she decided to destroy Sir Charles's apparatus. Sir Charles himself had been so cocksure of his success that he had never thought it necessary. She went down to Cornwall and I followed."

Again Sir Charles laughed. More than ever he looked a fine gentleman disgusted by a rat.

"Is some old chemical apparatus all your evidence?" he demanded contemptuously.

"No," said Poirot. "There is your passport showing the dates when you returned to and left England. They coincide with the period during which the butler, Ellis, was in Sir Bartholomew's service."

Egg had so far sat silent—a frozen figure. But now she stirred. A little cry, almost a moan, came from her.

Sir Charles turned superbly.

"Egg, you don't believe a word of this absurd story, do you?"

He laughed. His hands were outstretched.

Egg came slowly forward as though hypnotized. Her eyes gazed into his. And then, just before she reached him, she wavered, her glance fell, went this way and that, as though seeking for reassurance.

Then, with a cry, she fell on her knees by Poirot.

"Is this true? Is this true?"

He put both hands on her shoulders, a firm, kindly touch.

"It is true, mademoiselle."

Egg said:

"The other day, when we were in the country—all the time I felt afraid. I didn't know why. I was just afraid of something. Was that because—because——"

"Woman's intuition, my dear Egg," said Sir Charles, with a sneer.

He was still calm.

"This won't do, Poirot," he said. "I can explain the passport. It looks rather badly, I admit, but—well, there were reasons."

Hercule Poirot spoke in a brisk businesslike tone.

"In the next room, Sir Charles," he said, "are a Scotland Yard inspector and two doctors—eminent specialists in diseases of the brain."

"You've done that?" Sir Charles started forward. His face seemed to dissolve and re-form itself. It was now a leering mask of impotent fury. His voice rang shrill and cracked:

"You've trapped me! Yes, you've trapped me! I won't see them! This is a plot! It's a conspiracy! It's been closing round me! But they can't touch me—no one can touch me!" He drew himself up. "I'm above you all—above your silly man-made laws! Those three people had to be killed; it was a necessity! I regret their deaths, but it was necessary! It had to be! For my safety!"

He stopped and stared at Poirot, his jaw working.

"It's not true. It's a plant. A lie. There's no one there."

"See for yourself," said Hercule Poirot.

Sir Charles strode to the door, flung it open and passed through. They heard him give a shrill, high-pitched scream, and the low murmur of men's voices. Poirot went to the door, looked through and shut it carefully.

"It is all over, mademoiselle," he said. "He will be taken care of. And now, here is a friend to take you home."

He opened a second door and Oliver Manders came in. He went quickly over to Egg and she made a faltering step toward him.

"Oliver, I've been such a beast to you. Such a beast. Take me to mother! Oh, take me to mother!"

He put an arm round her and drew her toward the door.

"Yes, dear, I'll take you. Come."

"It's been so awful—so awful."

"I know. But it's all over now. You need never think of it again."

"I can't forget. I shall never forget."

"Yes, you will. You'll forget very soon. Come now."

She went with him obediently. At the door she took a hold on herself and disengaged herself from his arm.

"I'm all right now."

Poirot made a gesture and Oliver Manders came back into the room.

"Be very good to her," said Poirot.

"I will, sir. She's all I care about in the world; you know that. Love for her made me bitter and cynical. But I shall be different now. I'm ready to stand by. And some day, perhaps——"

"I think so," said Poirot. "I think she was beginning to care for you when he came along and dazzled her. Hero worship is a real and terrible danger to the young. Some day Egg will fall in love with a friend and build her happiness upon a rock."

He looked kindly after the young man as he left the room.

Mr. Satterthwaite leaned forward in his chair.

"M. Poirot" he said, "you have been wonderful—absolutely wonderful."

Poirot put on his modest look.

"It is nothing—nothing. A tragedy in three acts, and now the curtain has fallen."

"You'll excuse me," said Mr. Satterthwaite.

"Yes, there is some point you want explained to you?"

"There is one thing I want to know."

"Ask, then."

"Why do you sometimes speak perfectly good English and at other times not?"

Poirot laughed.

"Ah, I will explain. It is true that I can speak the exact, the idiomatic English. But, my friend, to speak the broken English is an enormous asset. It leads people to despise you. They say, 'A foreigner; he can't even speak English properly.' It is not my policy to terrify people; instead, I invite their gentle ridicule. Also I boast! An Englishman he says often, 'A fellow who thinks as much of himself as that cannot be worth much.' That is the English point of view. It is not at all true. And so, you see, I put people off their guard. Besides," he added, "it has become a habit."

"Dear me," said Mr. Satterthwaite. "Quite the cunning of the serpent, M. Poirot."

He was silent for a moment or two, thinking over the case.

"I'm afraid I have not shone over this matter," he said vexedly.

"On the contrary. You appreciated that important point—Sir Bartholomew's remark about the butler—you realized the astute observation of Miss Wills. In fact, you could have solved the whole thing if it had not been for your playgoer's reaction to dramatic effect."

Mr. Satterthwaite looked cheered.

Suddenly an idea struck him. His jaw fell.

"My goodness," he cried, "I've only just realized it! That rascal, with his poisoned cocktail! Anyone might have drunk it! It might have been me!"

"There is an even more terrible possibility that you have not considered," said Poirot.

"Eh?"

"It might have been me," said Hercule Poirot.